ira

15.9

ADAM'S FALL

BANTAM BOOKS BY SANDRA BROWN

ADAM'S FALL
FANTA C
A WHOLE NEW LIGHT
TEXAS! SAGE
22 INDIGO PLACE
TEXAS! CHASE
TEXAS! LUCKY

ADAM'S FALL

S A N D R A
B R O W N

BANTAM BOOKS

NEW YORK   TORONTO   LONDON   SYDNEY   AUCKLAND

ADAM'S FALL

A Bantam Book

PUBLISHING HISTORY
Bantam Loveswept edition published May 1988
Bantam hardcover edition/December 1993

BOOK DESIGN BY SIGNET M DESIGN, INC.

Library of Congress Cataloging-in-Publication Data
Brown, Sandra
    Adam's fall / Sandra Brown.
        p.   cm.
    ISBN 0-553-09538-2
    1. Man-woman relationships—United States—Fiction.   I. Title.
PS3552.R718A66   1993
813'.54—dc20   93-15495
                                                                               CIP

Published simultaneously in the United States and Canada

Bantam Books are published by Bantam Books, a division of Bantam
Doubleday Dell Publishing Group, Inc. Its trademark, consisting of the words
"Bantam Books" and the portrayal of a rooster, is Registered in U.S. Patent
and Trademark Office and in other countries. Marca Registrada. Bantam
Books, 1540 Broadway, New York,
New York 10036.

PRINTED IN THE UNITED STATES OF AMERICA

BVG   0 9 8 7 6 5 4

Dear Reader,

You have my wholehearted thanks for the interest and enthusiasm you've shown for my Loveswept romances over the past decade. I'm enormously pleased that the enjoyment I derived from writing them was contagious. Obviously you share my fondness for love stories which always end happily and leave us with a warm, inner glow.

Nothing quite equals the excitement one experiences when falling in love. In each romance, I tried to capture that excitement. The settings and characters and plots changed, but that was the recurring theme.

Something in all of us delights in lovers and their uneven pursuit for mutual fulfillment and happiness. Indeed, the pursuit is half the fun! I became deeply involved with each pair of lovers and their unique story. As though paying a visit to old friends for whom I played matchmaker, I often re-read their stories myself.

I hope you enjoy this encore edition of one of my personal favorites.

SANDRA BROWN

ADAM'S FALL

PROLOGUE

*I*T MADE THE EVENING NEWS.

The accident occurred on a mountain in northern Italy. As mountains went, it wasn't that majestic. But it was sufficient. Sufficiently high and rugged to win the respect of even expert climbers. A fall into a chasm of rock thirty feet deep was sufficient to seriously damage Adam Cavanaugh's spine, warrant headlines, and pitch hundreds of his employees around the globe into a panic.

Thad Randolph didn't panic. But the news report certainly gave him pause. He stopped repairing a Transformer for his son, Matt, and brusquely demanded quiet from him and his sister, Megan. Thad reached for the volume knob of the portable TV on the kitchen counter and turned it up.

". . . the only survivor. He has just been flown here to Rome, where the extent of his injuries will hopefully become known later this evening. Other members of the mountain climbing expedition party were French race car driver Pierre Gautier and English banking magnate Alexander Arrington. Both men were reported dead at the scene. Mr. Cavanaugh, an internationally renowned tycoon, is owner of the Hotel Cavanaugh chain. He is—"

"Hey, that's where Mom works," Matt said.

"Are they talking about the Adam we know?" Megan asked.

"Yes," Thad said grimly. "Shh."

The report was being broadcast live at the scene in Rome. The anchorman in New York asked the field reporter, "Are doctors speculating on Mr. Cavanaugh's condition at all?"

"No, they're not. Hospital officials refuse to release any information until Mr. Cavanaugh has undergone a thorough examination and his condition is fully ascertained. All we are being told at present is that his injury, or injuries, involve the spinal column and appear to be serious."

"Was he conscious when he arrived?"

"We've had no official confirmation of that, although he appeared not to be. As soon as the helicopter arrived, he was rushed inside. We'll have more information—"

Abruptly Thad reached for the sound knob and turned it all the way down. He said a word that his two children had been commissioned to ignore and forbidden to repeat. They never repeated it for fear of reprisal—which didn't seem quite fair since their mom never punished Thad for saying it—but they couldn't ignore it. Not when it practically sizzled off their dad's narrowed lips. "The damn fool."

"Who is?" Elizabeth Randolph entered the kitchen through the back door and dropped her briefcase and handbag on the table. The three of them swung around.

"Mom! Guess who the man on TV was talking about?"

"Matt, Megan, scoot," Thad said quickly. He made an arrow of his arm and pointed toward the door leading to the central rooms of the house.

"But, Dad—"

"Out. Let me talk to your mother alone."

"But she—"

The objections died on their lips when his eyebrows fashioned a steep V. He meant business. In the year since Thad Randolph had married Elizabeth Burke, her children had come to adore and respect him. He had adjusted to their rambunctiousness and they to his moods. They were affectionate with each other; the children had readily agreed to become his by adoption. But he was now wearing his no-nonsense face, which meant arguing would not only be ineffectual, but imprudent. They shuffled out.

"Thad? What is it?"

He moved toward Elizabeth and placed his hands on her shoulders. "I don't want you to get upset."

"The look on your face has already upset me. What's going on? What is it? What's happened? Something terrible, I know. Mom? Dad? Lilah?"

Elizabeth had lost her first husband to a dreadful freeway accident. She knew what it felt like to unexpectedly receive the worst of bad news. She felt again a sinking sensation in the pit of her stomach, just as she had the morning she'd opened her door to two policemen, holding their hats in their hands and wearing funereal expressions. Fearfully, she gripped the front of Thad's shirt.

"Tell me."

"It's Adam."

"Adam?" She wet her lips quickly. Her face turned pale.

Elizabeth was personally involved with Adam Cavanaugh. Originally it had been strictly a business arrangement. But their professional relationship had grown in proportion to the expansion of her Fantasy shops in the lobbies of Cavanaugh's hotels. The shops now totaled five with plans for more. Elizabeth and Adam shared a close personal friendship that at one time might have made Thad jealous. But since he was convinced that the handsome, young millionaire was no longer his rival for Elizabeth's love, Thad considered Adam his friend as well.

"Something's happened to Adam?" Elizabeth asked in a voice made thin by anxiety.

"He slipped and fell while mountain climbing in Italy."

"Oh, God." She pressed her fingers against her lips. "He's dead?"

"No. But he's seriously injured. They've taken him to Rome."

" 'Seriously injured'? How?"

"They're not sure of the extent of—"

"Thad."

He sighed with resignation. "Spinal injury."

Tears filled Elizabeth's eyes. "Was the spinal cord severed?"

"I don't know." When she looked dubious, he emphasized, "I swear, I don't know. The reports are sketchy." He told her everything the reporter had said. "It doesn't look good."

Elizabeth slumped against her husband. He embraced her tightly. "Adam was so looking forward to this trip," she said against the front of Thad's shirt. "When he told me he was going to climb that mountain, I said I thought he was crazy to risk life and limb on a silly sport." She sniffed back tears. "But I was only joking." She raised her head suddenly. "Two friends of his were going with him. What about them?"

Thad slid his fingers up into her hair and pressed her head back into place. He massaged her scalp. "They died in the accident, Elizabeth."

"Oh," she groaned, "how awful for Adam."

"According to the report, one of them slipped into an icy chasm and dragged the others down with him."

"Knowing Adam, whether it was his fault or not, he'll take full responsibility." After a moment she pushed herself away and looked up at Thad. "What should we do?"

"There's nothing we can do at this point."

"I've got to do something, Thad."

"You've got to think about yourself. And the baby." He laid his open hand against her lower abdomen, which was firmly rounded with pregnancy. She was in her last trimester. "Adam wouldn't want you to endanger his godchild."

"I could ask Mrs. Alder to come stay with the children. We could get a flight out of Chicago to Rome tonight."

"Uh-uh," he said, sternly shaking his head. "You're not flying to Rome."

"I can't just sit here and do nothing," she cried in frustration.

"You'll have plenty to do in the next few days. There'll be a million and one details to be taken care of. Everything will be in a state of chaos until Adam's prognosis is officially handed down. He would rely on your levelheadedness in such a crisis. You're far more valuable to him here, taking calls, staving off the curious, than you would be pacing the corridors of a Roman hospital, worrying about something you have no control over and wearing yourself out in the process."

She slumped dejectedly. "I guess you're right. I *know* you're right. It's just that I feel so useless."

Thad didn't say so, but he was thinking how much more useless Adam Cavanaugh was going to feel when he regained consciousness—God forbid that he wouldn't—and learned that he had suffered a debilitating spinal injury.

"The poor bastard," he muttered where Elizabeth couldn't hear, as he pulled her back into his reassuring embrace.

ONE

"*BAD IDEA. OF ALL IDEAS EVER CONCEIVED BY* man, this is the baddest."

Lilah Mason, standing in bare feet, skintight jeans, and a faded red T-shirt, looked like a commune mama straight out of the sixties. She'd been a mere child during that decade, but her expression personified the rebellious spirit of the bygone era. Vexed, she tossed her thick, curly hair over her shoulder. Wisps of blond bangs were held off her face by a bandanna sweatband tied around her forehead, but she made a reflexive swipe at them too.

"You haven't even heard us out yet," Elizabeth chided her younger sister.

"I heard enough. Adam Cavanaugh. That name is all I needed to hear to turn me against any plan you two have hatched." She eyed her sister and brother-in-law with open hostility. "Let's forget you ever mentioned it and go out for ice cream, okay? No hard feelings."

Thad and Elizabeth stared back at her with unspoken reproach. Seeing that they weren't yet willing to throw in the towel, Lilah flopped down on the sofa in the living room of her small apartment and drew one threadbare knee up in front of her like a shield. "Well, let's hear it. Give me the sermon quick so we can get it over with."

"He's not doing well, Lilah."

"Most patients with spinal injuries don't," she replied sarcastically. "Especially not at first. And most don't have the financial means to help themselves the way your Mr. Cavanaugh does. Thanks to his checkbook, he's got more doctors and nurses and physical therapists at his disposal than most patients in his condition could count. He doesn't need me."

"That's reverse snobbery, isn't it?" Thad asked her reasonably.

"How much money Cavanaugh does or does not have is irrelevant."

"Then why won't you agree to be his therapist?" Elizabeth demanded.

"Because I don't like him," Lilah shot back. She held up both hands to ward off the objections she saw rising from them. "No, let me rephrase that. I loathe and detest and despise him. And vice versa."

"That shouldn't have anything to do with it."

"Oh-ho, but it does!" Lilah bolted off the sofa and began pacing. "Guys like him who need physical therapy are the *worst*. I mean the absolute worst of patients. Children love and adore you for your attention. Elderly people are tearfully grateful to you for your kindness. Even young women are pathetically thankful. But men in Cavanaugh's age group," she said, shaking her head adamantly, "uh-uh. No way. We at the hospital draw straws to see who gets stuck with them."

"But Lilah—"

"Why is that?" Thad's voice overrode that of his wife. Elizabeth had a tendency to become emotional in situations such as this. His approach was more pragmatic, especially with his volatile sister-in-law, whose mood swings were drastic and unpredictable.

"Because for the most part they had been in great physical condition prior to the cause of their spinal trauma. Most are injured when participating in a dangerous sport. They're thrill-seekers. Active and adventurous. Motorcyclists, surfers, skiers, divers, that sort. They're athletically inclined. More so than the majority of the population. When one gets hurt and suffers paralysis, even temporarily, he goes a little wacko. He can't deal with going from superjock-superstud to helpless invalid. His psyche goes off the deep end. No matter how congenial he was before his accident, he becomes embittered by it and wants to punish everybody in the world for his misfortune. In short, he becomes a pain in the . . . neck."

"Adam won't be like that."

"Right," Lilah agreed drolly. "He'll be much worse. He had more to lose."

"He'll know you're there to help him."

"He'll resent everything I do."

"He'll thank you."

"He'll fight me."

"You'll be his ray of hope."

"I'll be his scapegoat." Lilah drew a long breath. "I would bear the brunt of his foul temper and his recalcitrance. *If* I subjected myself to that kind of abuse, which I won't. So, end of discussion. How about Häagen-Dazs?"

Elizabeth turned to Thad and looked at him in appeal. "Do something."

He laughed shortly and shrugged. "What do you want me to do? She's a grown woman. She makes up her own mind."

"Thank you, Thad," Lilah said righteously.

"But you saw Adam. I didn't." Thad had stood firm in his decision not to let Elizabeth fly abroad, but at her insistence he had gone to see Adam and had returned with a firsthand report on his condition. "Tell Lilah what the doctors said."

Sighing heavily, Lilah returned to her seat on the sofa. When she was settled, Thad told her, "I went to Hawaii to see him."

"I thought he was in Rome."

"He was. At his request he was transferred to a hospital in Honolulu after the surgery."

"He had surgery?" Thad nodded. "From what I understood, the spinal cord wasn't severed in the fall." Lilah's professional interest was piqued in spite of her personal aversion to the entrepreneur.

"Thank God it wasn't. But several bones in his back were broken or cracked. The surgeons repaired them. I don't know the medical jargon, but he suffered a spinal contusion. He had sustained a real blow to the spine that caused a lot of swelling."

"A contusion is a bruise. The tissue swells and puts pressure on the nerves. Until the swelling goes down, the doctors won't know for sure the extent of his paralysis or whether or not it's permanent."

"Exactly," Thad said, nodding at her knowledgeable summary, which agreed with what the experts had told him.

"And the surgery prolonged the time there would be swelling around the vertebrae," Lilah added.

"Yes, but that was two weeks ago. He should be showing improvement and he's not."

"He's still in a state of diaschisis?" At Thad's puzzled look she clarified, "Spinal shock. Paralysis."

"Yes."

"He doesn't feel any sensation below his waist?"

"None."

"He should have started therapy already." Thad looked away guiltily. "He has," Lilah said perceptively. "Hasn't he?"

"Yes," Thad mumbled grudgingly, "but he hasn't responded well."

"He's resisted it," Lilah stated flatly. "Which brings us full circle. You just made my point. Men like Adam always resent a therapist's interference. Mostly out of fear that they'll never be the same, they either want to do everything on their own, or they don't want to do anything at all. Which is it with Cavanaugh?"

"He doesn't want to do anything at all."

She gave a professional harrumph.

"Do you blame him?" Thad asked with a trace of exasperation.

Lilah snapped right back, "It's not my job to place blame, Thad. It's my job to make the best of what these patients have left. Not to baby them while they cry over what they've lost."

He ran a hand through his hair. "I know. I'm sorry. It's just, hell, if you could have seen him lying there in that damn bed, unable to move, looking so . . . pitiful."

Lilah's expression softened. "I see patients like that every day. Some much more pitiful than Adam Cavanaugh."

"I'm sure you do." Thad expelled a deep breath. "I didn't mean to suggest that Adam should take precedence over any other patient or that you aren't compassionate."

"It's just that Adam is our friend," Elizabeth said quietly. "Our very special friend."

"And my mortal enemy," Lilah reminded them. "From the first time we laid eyes on each other, it's been mutual detestation. You should remember, Lizzie. You introduced us that day in Fantasy."

"I remember."

"Remember your wedding? Adam and I could barely get through one obligatory waltz without coming to fisticuffs."

"He accused you of leading."

"I was! I didn't like the way he led." Elizabeth and Thad exchanged a glance. If the situation hadn't been so grave, they could have found humor in Lilah's account of their wedding reception. "And last Christmas morning as soon as I arrived at your house, he invented a lame, transparent excuse and left."

"Only after you made that wisecrack about the goose he brought."

"All I said was that for what he paid for the damn bird, one would think they'd've cut its head off."

"He took offense, Lilah," Elizabeth said. "And I don't blame him. The goose was a thoughtful gesture. It had been beautifully prepared by one of the hotel chefs and—"

"Ladies," Thad interrupted with a long-suffering sigh. When they fell silent, he addressed Lilah. "We're well aware of the ongoing antagonism between you and Adam. But we also think that, under the circumstances, personal considerations should be set aside."

"*My* personal considerations. As the therapist I have to be cajoling and nice to him. He can be a bastard to me and get away with it."

"Maybe so, Lilah, but we're talking about the man's life."

"He's still alive."

"Not to his way of thinking he isn't. We're talking quality of life here. You know what an ambitious, driven man Adam was. He was like an avalanche about to happen. He moved with the impetus of a steamroller."

"He could again," she argued. "The doctors have all but come right out and guaranteed that there's no permanent damage and that his paralysis is temporary."

"But Adam's not convinced. Until he is, it doesn't matter what the doctors tell him. He needs to be persuaded that his condition isn't permanent. And soon. One doctor told me that the longer he remains paralyzed, the less hope for a full recovery."

"That's right."

Elizabeth stood up and went to her sister. Sandwiching Lilah's hands between hers, she said, "Please, Lilah. I know it's asking a lot. But how bad can working in Hawaii be?"

"Unfair, Lizzie. Who can resist a job in Hawaii, much less a begging prego?"

Elizabeth smiled, but her eyes remained earnest. "Please."

"I'd have to take an indefinite leave of absence from my regular job." She was grasping at straws now, and all three knew it. Still, Lilah felt compelled to put up token resistance. "I'd be deserting my other patients in the middle of their therapy programs."

"There's an entire staff of capable therapists to take over for you."

"So hire one of them to work with this glorified bell-hop."

"None are as good as you."

"Flattery."

"You'd be getting paid triple what you're making now."

"Bribery."

"You'd come back with a fabulous tan."

"Coercion." After shooting them dirty looks, she thoughtfully gnawed on the inside of her cheek. "Be honest with me. How many therapists have tried with Cavanaugh and failed?"

"I'm not sure—"

"Three." Elizabeth, whose white lie had been shot down before it could take flight, turned to her husband with exasperation. "No sense in lying," he said with a shrug. "She would find out when she got there."

"But we'd have the Pacific Ocean between her and us when she found out."

Lilah laughed. "Three, huh? Good Lord, he's even worse than I thought. What were his objections to the therapists?"

"The first was a man," Thad told her. "Adam said his hands felt like hams with sledgehammers packed inside. Said he must have come straight from Rocky Balboa's training camp."

"Such a nice guy," Lilah said, exaggeratedly batting her eyelashes. "Go on."

"The second ran out of his room in tears. We're not sure what he said to her."

"*Her?* Young?" Thad nodded at Lilah's guess. "I can imagine. You'd be amazed at the lewd and imaginative propositions that are spouted from the mouths of paraplegics," she remarked. "What about the third one?"

Thad winced. "They tried another male. Adam claimed he was a, uh . . ."

"Homosexual," Lilah supplied.

"That kinda captures the gist of it, yeah."

Shaking her head, Lilah said, "The man is a classic case, I tell you, classic." She stood, slid her hands into the seat pockets of her jeans, and gave Thad and Elizabeth her back. She moved to the window and gazed through the open blinds. It was drizzling for the third straight day. Everything was autumnally gray. Hawaii would be a pleasant change of climate and scenery, certainly.

Was she *seriously* considering becoming physical therapist to Adam Cavanaugh, a man whose very name evoked shudders of dislike?

But he was still a patient, an accident victim, a seriously wounded man who might or might not walk normally again. A lot would depend on the extent of his injury. A lot would depend on the physical therapy he was given. And she was good in her field. She was exceptionally good.

She turned around to face Elizabeth and Thad. "Have you discussed this idea with the hospital staff in Honolulu?"

"Yes. They gave us the go-ahead."

"I'd have complete control over his therapy? I wouldn't have anyone questioning my methods, no stars-in-her-eyes nurse with a crush on him undoing my work, no one second-guessing or berating me?"

"What do you plan to do to the poor guy?"

Lilah smiled at Thad's suspicious inquiry. "If the doctors determine that he's capable of walking again, he'll hate me before he does. He'll set up a hue and cry and go through pure hell and so will I."

Elizabeth nervously clasped her hands over her swollen stomach. "You wouldn't . . . I mean, you and Adam don't like each other very much, but you wouldn't . . ."

"Deliberately hurt him?" Lilah asked angrily. "Give me some credit, Lizzie. I might not have many scruples, but my professional integrity is above reproach."

"Of course it is. Forgive me," Elizabeth said, rubbing her temples out of fatigue and distress. "I know you'll do the very best you can for Adam."

"I haven't said I will yet."

"Will you?"

"Who's paying me, him?"

"Actually his phalanx of subordinates is taking care of the bookkeeping, but the money comes out of Adam's personal account and not the corporation's."

"Good. He can afford me. One thousand dollars a day." At their shocked expressions, she said defensively, "Don't think I won't earn it. I'll earn twice that much. One thousand dollars a day plus my travel and living expenses in Hawaii."

"Agreed," Elizabeth said, knowing that she wouldn't have any difficulty justifying the expense to Adam's devoted staff.

"And he can't fire me. No one can fire me except you."

"All right. Are you formally accepting the position?"

Lilah rolled her eyes heavenward, said something that made Elizabeth glad she had opted to leave the children at home, and on a gust of air said, "Hell, yes. How can I resist having the mighty Adam Cavanaugh at my mercy?"

"There must be some mistake. Cavanaugh. C-a-v-a-n-a-u-g-h. First name Adam."

"I'm well aware of the name," the receptionist said condescendingly. "But as I've already told you, Mr. Cavanaugh has been released from this hospital."

Lilah shifted her heavy flight bag from one shoulder to the other. "The man is paraplegic. Don't tell me he walked out of here."

"I can't discuss a patient's condition."

"Then get someone down here who can. Pronto."

The receptionist did, but not pronto. It was forty-five minutes before the summoned doctor approached Lilah where she sat in the lobby like a miniature volcano about to blow its top. "Ms. Mason?"

Lilah tossed down the magazine she'd practically memorized during her wait. "Yes. Who are you?"

"Bo Arno."

"You're kidding."

" 'Fraid not. I'm sorry you were kept waiting so long." Though he grinned engagingly, Lilah didn't say anything to let him off the hook. His grin faltered. "If you'll come with me?"

He tried to take her suitcase, but she wouldn't let him. She lugged it and her shoulder bag into the elevator and remained ungraciously silent during the ride up to the sixth floor. Once seated in a chair in his office, she accepted his offer of a cold drink and nodded her thanks to the secretary who brought it to her. After one sip she demanded, "Is Adam Cavanaugh still in this hospital?"

"No, he isn't."

She cursed beneath her breath. "Then someone got his signals crossed. I was hired to be his personal therapist. I just flew across several time zones and the whole freaking ocean for nothing."

"We couldn't reach you in time, for which I apologize. Yesterday morning Mr. Cavanaugh demanded to be released. We had no recourse." He raised his hands in a helpless motion. "He's retreated to his home on Maui."

"What was his condition when he left?"

"Very poor. He's still flaccid. I begged him to wait until we knew more. He said he knew enough, said he was resigned to being a bedridden paraplegic the rest of his life, and insisted that he be transferred home. Frankly, Ms. Mason, I'm far more concerned about his mental state than I am about the diaschisis, which I firmly believe is temporary."

"The spine wasn't severed?"

"No. Traumatized drastically, but I believe when all the swelling goes down and he begins physical therapy, he'll gradually have sensation restored."

"Having sensation restored is a long way from climbing mountains. That's probably what Cavanaugh's thinking too."

"I'm sure you're right," the doctor replied with chagrin. "He wanted absolute guarantees from us, and from the specialists he had brought over from the mainland, that he would eventually be as he was before. None of us could give him unqualified answers. Often it's anybody's guess how these spinal injuries will heal and how ambulatory the patient will eventually be."

"Well, whether he could feel it or not, I'd like to give Mr. Cavanaugh a swift kick in the butt for wasting my time."

The doctor scratched his cheek absently. "I spoke with your sister, Mrs. Randolph. She suggested, and I concur, that you should follow Mr. Cavanaugh to Maui and begin therapy at once."

"Oh, she did, did she? Well, the next time you speak to my sister, give her this message for me." The message caused the cheek Dr. Arno was scratching to turn beet red. "Now, if you'll excuse me, Bo Arno, I'm going to find the hotel with the hottest shower and the firmest bed in the islands and crawl into both. Not necessarily in that order."

"Please, Ms. Mason." He popped out of his chair and gestured imploringly for her to return to hers. More out of weariness than obedience, Lilah sat back down. "If you live up to your credentials, this patient desperately needs you."

"And sharks need food. That doesn't mean I'm going to volunteer myself as dinner."

"It won't be that bad." She gave him a withering glance. He looked away first. "Granted," he said, squirming uncomfortably beneath her level blue gaze, "Mr. Cavanaugh is accustomed to having his own way. He can be difficult. But I'm certain you can handle him."

As he said that, he was taking in Lilah's white leather jacket, which was decorated with silver studs and a six-inch fringe. The coat was too warm for the climate, but she hadn't had a chance to take it off and it was easier to wear than to carry.

"Please, reconsider. Go to Maui."

"Are you familiar with the phrase 'No way, José'?"

Impatiently she listened as Dr. Arno earnestly recounted all the reasons Elizabeth and Thad had originally cited why she should agree to give Adam Cavanaugh physical therapy.

"Okay, okay!" she exclaimed so suddenly that the doctor jumped. "Right now I'd sell my soul for a bath. Which way's Maui and how do I get there from here?"

Sparing no expense, she itemized the equipment she wanted to take with her. While the doctor was making arrangements for it and a private plane to fly her to the other island, Lilah hailed a cab outside the hospital and went on a whirlwind shopping spree. She used the carte blanche expense account she'd been given to buy clothing more suitable to the climate.

By the time she alighted from the private plane on Maui, her slender figure was wrapped in a colorful sarong and she had sandals on her feet instead of boots. Using a wide-brimmed straw hat to shade her eyes, she searched for the rental car that she had been promised would be waiting for her.

Once behind the wheel, map in hand, she set out for Adam Cavanaugh's tropical retreat. The major highway soon narrowed to a minor one and eventually dwindled to a rutted dirt road that she cursed with each jolting lurch of the car. It wound it's way up a mountainside that was so verdantly rich, she couldn't help but be impressed by the wealth of unfamiliar vegetation.

She was also stunned by the sprawling estate that she discovered at the end of the climbing, twisting road. She had expected Adam Cavanaugh's house to be *nice*, but her destination surpassed her expectations. It was opulent.

A lava rock walkway led up to the mammoth front door made of frosted beveled glass. Hauling her luggage with her, she went toward it and pressed the button. Moments later the door swung open. At first she thought no one was there. But then her eyes dropped down to the tiny Asian man, whose wizened face was on a level with her midriff. Barely.

"Who you?"

"Little Bo Peep. I've lost my sheep. Also my marbles, or I wouldn't be here."

He thought that was hilariously funny and dissolved into knee-slapping laughter. "You Rirah?"

She laughed. "That's me. What's your name?"

"Pete."

"Pete! I was expecting something more Oriental."

"Doctor call. Say you come. Inside, inside." With amazing strength he took her suitcase from her and signaled her into a dazzling foyer floored in black and white marble squares.

She bent down and whispered to Pete, "Does the patient know I'm coming?" His wide grin collapsed. She had her answer. "I didn't think so. Where is he?" Pete's black eyes swung up to the gallery above them. "Up there?" He nodded solemnly. "Well, here goes nothing," she muttered.

Mentally hiking up her belt, she mounted the sweeping cantilevered staircase. Reaching the first door at the top, she paused and looked down questioningly at Pete. He shook his head and with quick jabbing thrusts of his index finger, pointed out another door. She went to it, silently inquired if she had the right one, and got an affirmative bob of his near-bald head before he turned and scampered off toward another part of the house.

"Chicken," she said beneath her breath.

Lilah's firm knock on the door was met with a bellow. "Go away." She knocked again. "Go away, dammit, are you deaf? I don't want any juice. I don't want a popsicle. I don't want a damn thing but to be left alone."

Lilah swung the door wide. "Tough tittie."

Adam's mouth dropped open in astonishment. Once he'd convinced himself that she wasn't a nightmare, his head hit the pillow behind it with a defeated plop. He laughed mirthlessly. "God, I must have done some serious sinning to find myself in this hell."

"Hello to you too."

The soles of her new sandals slapped against the glazed tile floor as she made her way toward the rented hospital bed. She didn't stop until she was standing at the foot of it, where she allowed the belligerent patient to give her a once-over.

Sneering with derision, he said, "Most women would have better taste than to dangle a salad bar from their ears."

Lilah shook her head, jangling the plastic fruit clusters she'd bought on one of Honolulu's commercial drags that catered to tourists. "I thought these earrings were kinda cute."

"Oh, it's a great costume, but Halloween's already passed."

By an act of will Lilah withheld a scalding comeback. Instead she closed her eyes and counted to ten, mumbling, "Just as I thought. This was a real bad idea."

TWO

"*WHAT THE HELL ARE YOU DOING HERE?*"

"I go out of my way to visit sick friends. It's one of my virtues."

"You don't have any virtues. I doubt you have any friends. And if you do, I doubt you're that conscientious about paying sick calls."

She made a tsking sound. "My, my, aren't we in a nasty mood today."

Adam drew his sleek dark brows into a fierce scowl. "I have every right to be in a nasty mood," he snarled. "My last two weeks would make the Hundred Years War look like a festival. I've been at the mercy of quacks whose stock answer to every question is, 'We'll have to wait and see.' I've been the hapless victim of despotic nurses who've taken delight in bossing me, poking me, sticking tubes into orifices I didn't even know I had, and feeding me garbage for food. The parts of my body that still have sensation have been in tremendous pain. I think I've got bedsores on my backside. I know I've got a blister on my tongue." He paused to draw in a deep breath. "And to top it all off, *you* show up. Which brings me around to my original question. What the hell are you doing here?"

"I needed to use your shower," she said cheekily. "Excuse me."

"Don't you give me that— Hey, where— Come back here, Mason. *Mason!*"

Lilah left him yelling her name. She leaned against the door she pulled closed behind her. When the drinking glass struck it, her ears absorbed the full impact of shattering glass. She whistled and through the door called, "Wow, you're really ticked, aren't you?"

She went downstairs and following her nose, found Pete in a kitchen that had a picture window as large as a movie-theater screen. It offered a spectacular view of the mountainside in the near distance and the Pacific Ocean on the far horizon.

"Are you a masochist or what?" she asked. Pete looked at her in confusion, holding aloft a butcher knife with which he had been slicing vegetables faster than her eyes could move. "Never mind. Where'd you put my bags?"

Smiling happily, Pete left his work in the kitchen and escorted her upstairs again. "Right next door," he said, nodding toward the room where Adam was.

"Yippee."

"You don't rike room?"

When she saw that Pete was crestfallen, she hastily inverted her sarcastic frown into a smile. "No, the room is terrific. Really."

She stepped past him and entered a guest bedroom suite that was twice as large as her whole apartment. It was better equipped, too, having a small refrigerator with an automatic icemaker, a two-burner cooktop, and a wet bar in addition to the black marble bathroom that was positively hedonistic. "I knew I should have gone into the hotel business," she muttered as she ran her fingers over teal-green towels that were as plush as expensive carpet.

" 'Xcuse?"

"Nothing, Pete. I was just being covetous. When's dinner?"

"Eight o'clock."

She consulted her wristwatch and mentally accounted for the time zones she'd flown through. "That gives me time for a bath and a nap. Wake me up at seven-thirty." He bobbed his head rapidly. "How long has it been since Mr. Cavanaugh had a meal?"

"Not since come home."

"That's what I thought. He's not eating anything?" Pete shook his head. "Fix him a dinner tray."

"Won't eat. Throw on floor."

"Not this time, he won't," she said, her eyes gleaming with determination. "Oh, by the way, a courier should be delivering some equipment here this afternoon. If the van can make it up that goat path," she added as an aside. "And there's a broken glass in Prince Cavanaugh's room that needs to be swept up."

Pete wanted to unpack for her, but she shooed him out so she could avail herself of the bathtub with the built-in whirlpool. Sprawling on the king-size bed and pulling the satin sheet over her naked body, she fell instantly asleep. She would have liked at least another eight hours when the funny little servant knocked on the door, then entered carrying a glass of chilled pineapple juice on a silver tray.

"Thanks," she said after draining the juice in one swallow. "I'll be down shortly." Pete scuttled out. Lilah dropped the sheet and regretfully left the bed. "Later," she told it, giving the satin sheets a lover's pat.

No one would blame her if she waited until the following morning to commence the physical therapy program with Adam Cavanaugh. This had been a hellish day, especially following her long trip. But she was being paid well for this job. Never let it be said that Lilah Mason had taken advantage of the sybaritic surroundings without giving full attention to her patient.

Besides, now that she was here, she was actually anxious to begin. Adam's condition, along with his negative state of mind, were challenges that she, as a professional, couldn't resist tackling. Even the slightest improvement in a patient was often reason for celebration. Adam needed the encouragement that came with accomplishing a small goal.

Then, too, the longer his muscles remained flaccid,

without sensation or the ability to move, the less likelihood of a full recovery. By now he should have experienced some sensation in those muscles. Lilah couldn't afford to wait any longer to begin his therapy even if she wanted to.

With that sobering thought in mind, she left her suite wearing the same Hawaiian ensemble she had had on when she arrived, sans the straw hat. Pete insisted that she eat her dinner in the dining room, though she sat alone at the glass table decorated with burning tapers in crystal holders and a lavish bouquet of orchids. The stir-fry vegetables and fish were delicious. She complimented Pete on the meal as he followed her upstairs carrying a dinner tray for the patient.

At Adam's bedroom door she took the tray from him. "If I don't come out alive, you have my permission to smother him in his sleep."

"Won't rike," Pete said, looking fearfully toward the closed door.

"Probably not, but it's only going to get worse before it gets better," she told him as she signaled with her head for him to open the door for her. "Best get started and get it over with." As soon as she had cleared the door, Pete closed it firmly.

Adam was listlessly gazing out the window. He rolled his head toward the door and groaned when he saw her. "Go away."

"No way. Hey, that rhymes. I'm a poet and didn't know it."

The look he sent across the room was murderous. "Is Elizabeth responsible for your being here?"

"You don't think I'd come voluntarily, do you?"

"I thought Elizabeth was my friend."

"She is. She wants to do what's best for you."

He barked a bitter laugh. "If you're the best, God help me should they decide to do the worst."

"If it were up to me, I'd let you lie here and rot in your own self-pity." She shrugged. "But you've got lots of money and some of it will come my way if I stay here and give you physical therapy."

"Like hell!" he shouted.

"The accommodations here are fair to middling. The job includes a Hawaiian vacation that I can certainly use. Back home it's cold and rainy, and my tan needs refreshing. What a relief to get away from my regular job. I was working with a patient who is an even bigger jerk than you are . . . and if you throw that napkin on the floor one more time, Mr. Cavanaugh, I'll bloody well throw you down there to pick it up."

Standing with hands on hips beside his bed, she glared down at him. He returned her animosity measure for measure. "Take this tray and your ridiculous bedside manner and shove them both up—"

"I've heard it," she interrupted. "There's not an original insult or abusive phrase that I haven't heard. No matter how obscene, they don't faze me. So save your energy and my time and start eating your dinner. Because you're going to eat it before I leave this room. The sooner you do the former, the sooner I do the latter. It comes down to how long you can tolerate my company."

She set the bed tray across his lap and plopped down on the bed beside him, folding her arms across her middle. The motion plumped her breasts up and out, causing them to swell above the fabric of the strapless sarong. She watched the patient's eyes lower to her chest, but she didn't alter her position. Her expression remained impassive when he insolently raised his eyes back to hers.

"Does a view of your cleavage go with your services?"

"Fringe benefit," she replied with a cheeky smile, "thrown in for free."

"I've seen better."

"Not at this price, you haven't."

"What are you being paid? I'll double it to get you out of here."

"I figured you'd try that." She fished in the bowl of fruit salad on his dinner tray and came up with a pineapple spear. She sucked on it nonchalantly. "But you might as well know right off the bat that money isn't my only motive."

"Don't tell me you came here out of the goodness of your heart."

She made a face at him. "You know better than that."

"Then what?"

"Imagine what a boost it will be to my career to work with the great Adam Cavanaugh. Pretty soon offers will come rolling in from movie stars with lower back syndrome and sports stars with stress injuries. Before it's over, I'll be as famous as you."

"You're wasting your time. I'll never be good for anything but to lie here and stare at the ceiling."

"Wanna bet, duckie? I'll have you walking if it kills me. If it kills both of us. In the meantime we're going to come to hate each other."

"We already hate each other."

She laughed. "So we're ahead of the game. Now be a good boy and eat these nice, plump veggies Pete has cooked for you."

"I'm not hungry."

"You've got to be. You haven't eaten in days. Pete said so." She picked a slice of banana out of the fruit salad and ate it. "He cringes every time your name is mentioned. What did you do to terrorize him, anyway?"

"I told him I was on speaking terms with Buddha and that he'd never reach nirvana if he didn't get out of here and stop pestering me. And the same goes for you."

"No good. I'm not a Buddhist."

"You know what I mean." He turned his head away. "Just get away from me. Leave me alone."

"Not till you've had dinner."

"You can't force me to eat."

"And you can't force me to leave. You can't move, remember?"

His eyes narrowed dangerously. "Get out." He strained the words through a set of straight, white teeth.

"Not until I've given you all the expertise I've got. So that when I'm interviewed by *People* magazine I'll be able to say in all honesty, and with an eloquent little tear in my eye, that I did everything possible for you." She spread the linen napkin over his bare chest. "Nice pecs. They'll come in handy when you start moving yourself into the wheel-chair. Nice chest hair too. Very sexy."

"Go to hell."

"At the risk of repeating myself, not until you've eaten your dinner." She held a forkful of food near his mouth. He refused to open it. "Look, Ace, you're in a state of malnutrition already. Because of the atrophy of muscle and bone, you've got negative nitrogen balance, which means bad news. Unless you get some protein into your tissues, you're history. Besides that, if you pack some meat on those bones, they won't protrude so much, which is one reason you've got decubitus ulcer, or in layman's terms, bedsores on your backside.

"Now, I know you can digest because Bo Arno told me you could. You've also regained bowel and urinary control, which came as a great relief to me, and which is one reason I'm trying to talk you into eating a full meal. Otherwise, I would pretend I didn't notice that you were starving to death in addition to your osteoporosis, soft tissue ossifica-tion, contracture, etcetera that goes with lying around and not doing anything.

"To sum it up, Cavanaugh, you're dead in the water before we start unless you eat some of this food. Now, what'll it be?"

He stared at her, then at the fork she still held near his mouth. "My arms aren't paralyzed. I can feed myself."

"Good. That's one less duty I'll have to worry about."

She passed him the fork. He looked at it for another long moment. Then crammed it into his mouth. It became apparent just how hungry he was. After that first bite, he ate ravenously, practically shoveling in the food. Because he was so busy chewing and swallowing, Lilah handled the conversation almost single-handedly.

"I don't know when you saw Elizabeth last, but baby has really blossomed in the last few weeks. Elizabeth is as wide as a barn and her boobs are out to here." She made a motion with her hands, cupping air several inches in front of her chest. "Thad's giddy over them. She's convinced baby is going to come early, though her doctor says everything's right on schedule. They've gotten the nursery painted and ready. All it needs is an occupant.

"Megan, of course, can't wait to have the baby home so she can help take care of it. I want to see her the first time she's confronted with a dirty diaper. Bet her tune will change fast enough. That was an awfully indelicate belch, Cavanaugh. More water?

"Matt's afraid they're going to love the baby more than they love him, so he's being a real pill, and Elizabeth is letting him get by with it so as not to unbalance his psyche. Thad is acting like a complete dodo. For a man his age his daddyhood antics border on the absurd. But this is his first child, so I guess it's understandable if one is into that kind of thing."

"What kind of thing?" Adam mumbled around a mouthful.

"You know, home and hearth."

"That's not for you?"

"Hardly!"

"You don't envy your sister?"

"Are you kidding?"

"You'd rather sleep around."

"What a tacky phrase, Mr. Cavanaugh," she said, taking umbrage. "I read the newspapers, same as you. I know what's going on. Nobody in his right mind 'sleeps around' anymore."

"That must really cramp your style."

"On the contrary," she said coldly. "I've always been very particular about my bed partners."

"But you've never narrowed the number down to one."

"I think settling down with one man for life sounds *boring*." He harrumphed and blotted his mouth with the napkin, then tossed it down into the empty plate. "You missed the tapioca," Lilah pointed out, pleased to see that it was all that was left of the food.

"I despise tapioca and Pete knows it. That's his way of defying me."

"What are you going to do about it," she taunted, "beat him up?"

"Very funny." He closed his eyes and laid his head on the pillow. "All right, I've eaten. Get lost."

"Oh, I can't. Not for a while."

His eyes popped open. "You said you'd leave me alone if I ate."

"Well, I fudged a smidgen. Now, don't look so venomous. We're just getting to the fun part."

"Somehow I doubt that."

She lifted the tray off his lap and set it on the floor near the door, which she opened. "Pete, we're ready," she called. Her voice echoed through the house.

"Ready for what? Look, I ate, isn't that enough?"

"Nope. We start tonight."

"Start what?"

"A smoldering affair." Adam raised startled eyes. She laughed. "Don't you wish? Actually we start your physical therapy."

"I don't want physical therapy. It won't do any good. I'm not putting myself through that humiliation. Pete, get that crap out of here. What's in those boxes?"

"Portable therapy equipment."

"Get it out of here."

"Soon this bedroom will look like a gymnasium. Hand me that screwdriver, will you, Pete?"

"Pete, if you value your job, if you value your Asian ass, you won't lift a hand to— All right, you're fired. Pete, didn't you hear me?" Then in a stubborn tone of voice, "I won't use any of this. I mean it, you two. You're wasting your time."

"Will you shut up!" Lilah yelled at him as she rammed the screwdriver into the palm of her hand. "Look what you made me do."

"This is my house," Adam said in a tightly controlled voice. "I didn't ask for your services, Ms. Mason. I don't want them. I don't want you."

"Well, you've got me."

"You're fired."

"Didn't I mention that you can't fire me? No? Oh, that was part of the deal. Pete, hold this trapeze in place while I secure it to the wall. A little higher. There."

Adam fumed while she, with Pete's assistance, set up the trapeze and two pulleys behind his bed. "That'll do for now," Lilah said, stepping back to review their handiwork. "We won't need the other stuff until later, so just leave it downstairs for the time being. Thanks, Pete." She kissed his balding pate. "You can close the door on your way out."

"You've gone to a lot of trouble for nothing," Adam said after Pete had withdrawn.

"I know guys who would dearly *love* to have a trapeze installed over their beds." Far from smiling, he glowered more intensely. Lilah sighed. "So much for levity. By using this trapeze, you can shift your weight and relieve pressure off any one spot. Unless you've grown fond of those bedsores." She smiled teasingly, but his face remained stony. "And anytime you want, you can exercise your upper torso and arms with the pulleys. That'll accomplish two things. It'll exercise you so you'll get tired and sleep better, and it'll give you an appetite. If you get bored with the pulleys, I can bring you some dumbbells."

"Which is what you must think I am. A dumbbell. I won't bother myself with this. It's futile. I just want to—"

"Pout. Feel sorry for yourself. Sulk. Wallow in self-pity because you've finally found something that money can't buy."

"Yes!" he hissed. "And why not?" Angrily he gestured down at his motionless legs beneath the sheet. "Look at me."

"I was about to," Lilah said calmly. Before he was prepared for it, she whipped back the sheet.

Adam sucked in a startled breath. So did Lilah, though she managed to hide it. She'd seen bodies by the hundreds in every shape, size, and condition. She'd never seen one this well made. It was proportioned like Michelangelo's *David*. But much more virile. And tanned. And garnished with soft, dark body hair that she wanted to test for softness.

It was obvious that he'd missed several days' meals. His ribs were individually delineated. It was obvious that before his accident he had been athletically active. The muscles of his thighs and calves were well defined. It was also obvious that he could satiate even the most demanding woman.

"Very nice," Lilah said with a studied air of indifference. "I can see why you're upset that such nice muscles are no longer working for you." She draped a white gym towel over his lower abdomen. "Let's get started."

"Doing what?"

"What the other three therapists tried to do before you scared them off. I'm going to take each joint through a passive exercise, rotating each one to the extent of its range."

"You're right. They all did that. It's a waste of time."

"My time. Hardly wasted because I'm being paid so well for it. And you haven't got anything else to do. So you might as well lie back and keep your mouth shut."

He summed up in two terse gutter words what he'd like to happen to her. She frowned down at him. "You're in no shape to do that either. Sorry. You're missing a real treat. And I'm afraid that once you're capable of it, you won't want me. If you think you hate me now, wait until we get to PNF."

"What the hell is that?"

"Physioneurologic facilitation."

His eyes sparked with dark fire. "That sounds dirty."

"It's nothing to look forward to, believe me. But for right now, passive exercise will do. Tonight, we'll keep you on the bed. But tomorrow morning, we'll start standing exercises and then moving you to the mat table."

"Standing exercises?"

"On the tilt table. I know you're already familiar with it, so don't pull a dumb act on me."

"I hate that damn thing."

"It's not much fun, I'll grant you that. But you don't want your blood to pool, do you? Besides, standing aids in urinary drainage. I'd hate for you to have to go back to a catheter because while you're supine that can cause infection, stone formation, and vesicourethral reflux."

"Can we talk about something else?" he asked, his face turning pale.

"Sure. What do you want to talk about?"

"Nothing."

Standing beside the bed, Lilah took his right foot between her hands and began rotating the stiff ball joint. "How often has Pete been turning you?"

"He hasn't."

"You wouldn't let him."

"That's right. It's humiliating."

"You're supposed to be turned every two hours."

"Yeah, yeah."

"No wonder you've got bedsores on your backside. What good are you doing yourself if you won't let people help you?"

"I'm used to helping myself."

"A self-reliant, macho man."

"What's wrong with that?"

"Under the circumstances it's a stupid, counterproductive attitude to take. But," she rushed on when she saw he was about to take issue, "if you want to be self-reliant, then you can learn to turn yourself in bed." Seeing that she had his interest, she explained, "That's where the trapeze will come in handy. If you're self-conscious about using it, I suggest you practice when no one is around. Feel anything?"

"No."

She moved around the end of the bed and took his other foot between her hands. "Want to talk about it?"

"What?"

"The accident."

"No."

"I'm sorry about your friends."

"So am I," he said quietly, closing his eyes. "But maybe they're better off than I am."

"What a stupid thing to say. Do you honestly think that you'd be better off dead?"

"Yes," he said bitingly. "Better that than being a useless lump for the rest of my life."

"Who says you will be? Your spinal cord wasn't severed. I know people who've had theirs severed and they're far from useless. They're productive human beings with jobs and families. It's all in the attitude you take."

"Does this lecture cost extra?"

"No, it's thrown in for the stupid, for the ignorant, for those with bad attitudes. Your prognosis for a full recovery is very good, though it might be a long time in coming."

"But not guaranteed."

She tilted her head to one side and eyed him knowledgeably. "None of us is guaranteed tomorrow, Cavanaugh. Besides, from what Elizabeth tells me, you're a gambler. Not only do you relish taking life-threatening risks like mountain climbing, but business risks as well. Didn't you, against the advice of your board, recently buy out a floundering chain of hotels in the Northwest? And hasn't that chain turned itself around?"

"Luck."

"Don't you feel lucky anymore?"

"Would you?" he challenged.

"Yeah. Lucky I wasn't renting space in a coffin."

He cursed lavishly and turned his head away. "How much longer is this going to take?"

"Could be weeks. Months maybe."

"I mean this. This . . . what you're doing now."

"An hour."

"Damn."

"Does it hurt?"

"No. I wish it did."

"So do I, Adam."

His head snapped around and he shot her a hard look. "Don't you dare pity me."

"Pity?" she said, laughing shortly. "I wouldn't think of it. You've got enough self-pity. You're oozing the stuff. You sure as hell don't need mine."

Methodically she went through the regimen. His mind seemed detached from his body. He had no connection with it. What hadn't been shut off by his accident, he had shut off deliberately. Most of the time he kept his eyes closed and his head averted, taking no interest in what she was doing. When he looked at her, it was with unmitigated hostility.

"That's enough for tonight," she said at last. "There is some constriction, especially in the lower extremities, but that's because they've been neglected since you left the hospital and is not a result of your accident."

"Thank you, Marcus Welby. Now, will you get your tush out of here and leave me in peace?"

"Sure. I'm exhausted."

"Take all that junk with you." He nodded toward the metal trolley Pete had rolled in earlier.

"What, that?" Lilah asked innocently. "That stays. We'll need it tomorrow."

She removed the gym towel and re-covered him with the sheet. As she was bending over him to straighten it, he caught her forearms. His fingers and hands had seemingly suffered no loss of muscle control, flexibility, or strength. His grip was surprisingly hard.

"You want me to feel something?" he asked silkily. "Then why don't you do the physical therapy you do best?"

"Which is?"

The smile that had caused hearts all over the world to patter spread across his lips. He dropped one eyelid in a suggestive wink. "Come on, Lilah. Hot little tart that you are, I'm sure you can think of something that would be good for me, a trick guaranteed to raise even a dead man. Why don't you straddle my lap and see the extent of range you get."

"Let me go."

He didn't. Instead he gripped her arms tighter and drew her down closer to him. "I've been lying here watching you sashay back and forth like you owned the place. I've listened to your irritating, nonsensical chatter till I'm sick of it. That smart mouth of yours is bound to be good for something besides making wisecracks. Let's see just how good you are at your job."

He yanked her down and kissed her hard. His tongue speared through her lips and plumbed her mouth with sleek, expert precision. He slid one hand around the back of her neck while his other moved to her breast. He kneaded it through the strapless bodice of the sarong, then pushed his hand inside and rubbed his fingertips back and forth across her nipple.

Lilah wrested herself free and backed out of his reach. She pulled her dress back into place and shook her hair over her shoulders as she squared them. Her mouth was wet and red from his kiss. She licked her lower lip. It felt swollen and bruised. And it tasted wonderful.

That unnerved her more than anything.

"It's going to take more than lewd propositions to scare me off, Mr. Cavanaugh. That kind of behavior is juvenile and unoriginal. It's characteristic of a healthy man who suffers an accident like yours to become an abusive sexist only to prove to himself that he's still a man. Be as disgusting and decadent as you want. It'll reflect on your character, not mine."

Furiously, he pounded the mattress with his fists. "Why'd they send you? *You?* I mean—dear God!—you top the list of people I would least rather have around."

"Vice versa, pal, but for as long as it takes, you're stuck with me."

"When this is all over," he said in a voice so menacing it sounded like a growl, "I'll personally kick you out of my house and back to the mainland."

Lilah's eyes twinkled. "I thought you said you'd always be a useless lump." She laughed at his whey-faced expression when he realized he had trapped himself. "Look at it this way. Kicking me back to the mainland will give you something to work toward. Nighty-night, Ace."

THREE

*A*DAM'S SUGGESTION HADN'T BEEN ALL THAT unappealing. That bothered her. When he had invited her to straddle his lap, the idea had struck her as being erotic rather than crude.

Male patients commonly made obscene remarks and propositions as a means of venting their frustration. Ordinarily she dismissed the lewd comments with a chastising put-down or a flippant joke seconds after they were uttered. Yet, almost ten hours later, Adam's words were still echoing through her mind. Disturbing.

Not only disturbing, but farfetched. How could a man who couldn't even move, move her?

Why did it seem that all her senses were more finely tuned this morning? Perhaps it was the tropical setting. Bali Ha'i didn't hold a candle to Cavanaugh's mountain retreat. The landscape was gorgeous, the colors vivid, the climate balmy, the air perfumed with the heady fragrance of Polynesian blossoms. The house was an architectural triumph that maximized the vistas beyond its stucco walls and enormous windows. The decor was harmonious but eclectic, reflecting Adam's variety of interests and tastes.

Luxurious as they were though, Lilah didn't think her surroundings were solely responsible for her sensual awareness. On the other hand, it was untenable to think that Adam Cavanaugh might be.

She didn't like him. Not at all. When Elizabeth had first expressed an interest in him, Lilah had warned her about such smooth operators. He was accustomed to ordering "Jump!" and a whole corps of subordinates would jump. Not only his bankroll, but his natural charm and Hollywood good looks had lured scores of cosmopolitan women to his side. He was a playboy. His newsworthy romantic liaisons were enough to make Lilah snicker with contempt. Men like Adam Cavanaugh had certainly never held any appeal for her.

Granted, Adam did have a few virtues to his credit. He generously supported numerous charities. He'd acted as knight in shining armor to Elizabeth by personally financing the expansion of her Fantasy shops. Without his assistance Elizabeth would have never ventured into such risky but potentially rewarding waters.

Aside from that, however, Lilah had always been suspicious of him. As she had told Elizabeth, she mistrusted anyone as polished as he. He must have a personality flaw that was as ruinous as a deep fault in a seemingly perfect diamond.

So why did her stomach go all aquiver whenever she thought about his kiss? When she had whipped that sheet back, she had wanted to impress him with how blasé she was toward the nude male body. Well, her plan had backfired. It turned out that she was the one who had been impressed. And in the wrong way.

Through the night she had gone into his room at two-hour intervals to turn him. The first time her efforts had been met with vile cursing and name-calling. She had ignored it and forced him onto his side. "Comfy?"

"Go to hell."

"Good night."

"Go to hell."

The next time her alarm went off and she stumbled into his room, he was moaning in his sleep. "Adam?" she asked softly. She rolled him to his back. There were tears on his cheeks.

"Pierre?" he called fretfully. "Alex? Answer me. *God, no!* I can't find them. Why aren't they saying anything?"

She turned him to his other side, adjusted the sheet, and withdrew without his ever awakening from his nightmare. She didn't leave until his tortured monologue had ceased and his breathing had become regular. He slept, or pretended to sleep, through the other times she had turned him. Each time she touched his warm skin she experienced a sensation, not unlike light-headedness, in her lower abdomen.

Crazy. For her to get jelly-kneed over any man. But *Adam Cavanaugh*? Crazy.

Pulling on white shorts and a white T-shirt with a huge red hibiscus flower silk-screened on the front, she left her bedroom. "God bless you, Pete," she told him when she entered the kitchen and her nose picked up the aroma of freshly brewed coffee. Grinning from ear to ear, he poured her a cup and passed it to her. She shook her head at his offer of cream and sugar and sipping at the steaming coffee, sat down at the bar.

"Ham, eggs, pancakes?" he asked.

"No, thanks. The fruit looks good." He'd been arranging slices of mango, papaya, and pineapple on a platter when she came in. "And a slice of wheat toast, please. Any word from upstairs?"

"Use bedpan. Say, 'I don't rike pee in pan no more.' "

Lilah laughed while she ate her light breakfast. "Good. Maybe that'll inspire him to get into a wheelchair so he can use the bathroom." She dusted toast crumbs off her hands. "Thanks for the breakfast. Time to attack. Is his tray ready?" She declined Pete's assistance and carried the tray up herself. Knocking once, she immediately pushed open the door.

"Good morn—" The second syllable died on her lips. She barely managed to set the tray on a credenza before rushing across the room toward Adam's bed. "Lord, what is it?"

His face was twisted with agony. His lips were thin and white and stretched open to reveal clenched teeth. "Left thigh. Cramp," he gasped.

Lilah flung back the sheet and gave his left thigh a cursory examination. The instant she touched the contracted muscle she said, "Spasticity." Her capable hands massaged the leg muscle. Adam cried out twice.

"Do you want a pain pill?"

"No. I hate not being in control of my own mind."

"Don't be proud. If you need a pain pill—"

"No pills," he shouted.

"Fine," she shouted right back. Thankfully her touch was kinder than her tone of voice. She continued to massage his thigh. Finally the muscle began to relax and with it, his grimace of pain.

"Thanks," he said, opening his eyes slowly. "Damn. That was . . . What are you grinning at?"

"Are you dense? That's a good sign, you idiot. The muscles aren't flaccid anymore."

He stared up at her for a moment. When the reason for her smile registered with him, he reciprocated with a wide one of his own. "What does the spasticity mean?"

"It probably means that the swelling has gone down and relieved the pressure around the vertebrae affecting those muscles. Can you feel this?" She pinched his bare thigh.

He gave her a baleful look. "It's a good thing for you that all I feel is pressure, no pain."

"But you can feel the pressure?" He nodded. "How about here?" She squeezed the muscle above his knee.

"No."

"Here?" She ran her finger up the sole of his foot.

"Nothing."

"Don't look discouraged. The sensation will start in your thighs and work down. How about your right thigh?" She scratched it lightly with her fingernails. He said nothing. When she raised inquisitive eyes toward him, he was staring at the spot where her hand was resting high on his thigh.

"Pressure," he said gruffly, reaching for the sheet and pulling it up. Lilah turned away quickly.

"Great. That's terrific news. Although it means that you'll be quite uncomfortable when those muscles contract. We'll be spending more time together, working harder and more often." She went on with brisk efficiency. "I'll have to notify Arno. He'll want to examine you. I'll call him while you're eating." She bridged his lap with the bed tray and left the room before he could say anything more.

When she got to her bedroom, which Pete had already straightened in her brief absence, she reached for the telephone on the nightstand and dialed a number. But it wasn't Dr. Arno in Honolulu who answered.

"Hi, Thad, it's Lilah."

"Hi! How are you? Trip go okay?"

"Don't you dare pull this buddy-buddy act with me. I don't feel like being civil. I'm furious with you."

"Furious? With me?"

"You were no doubt in on the conspiracy."

"What conspiracy is that, Lilah?"

"You know damn well what conspiracy. The one you and my big sister cooked up to have me stranded on an island with this generation's equivalent to Conrad Hilton."

"Hardly stranded. And hardly just 'an island.' I hear Maui's beautiful. I've always wanted to go there. Maybe next summer we can take the kids—"

"Thad!" After counting to ten Lilah said tensely, "I've had second thoughts. I don't want this lousy job. He's horrible. Awful. Worse than I expected. He's been verbally and physically abusive."

"Physically? How can a paralyzed man be physically abusive?"

He kissed me till my ears rang. She didn't say that, of course. She stammered around an answer and finally came up with, "He threw a drinking glass at me."

"And hit you with it?! Elizabeth, come here. It's Lilah. Adam threw a glass at her."

Lilah heard shuffling sounds as the receiver was transferred to her sister's hand. She also heard Matt's wailing in the background, "I wanna talk to Aunt Lilah." He was shushed by both parents. Finally Elizabeth's worried voice reached her. "Adam threw a glass at you? That doesn't sound at all like something he would do."

Lilah cursed beneath her breath, then parroted her sister's sentence in a mocking voice. "I told you, Lizzie. When something like this happens to a man, his whole personality undergoes a change. At least temporarily. And

usually for the worse. I didn't like Cavanaugh to begin
with. I sure don't like him now."

"If he threw a glass, you must have provoked him. What
did you do?"

"Thanks a lot!"

"Well, I know better than anybody how outrageous you
can be, Lilah."

"I've been strictly professional. I haven't done one outrageous thing since I got here." She thought about the
salad bar earrings and the theatrical way she'd unfurled the
bedsheet, but decided that, all things considered, what she
told her sister was basically the truth.

"The man is impossible. This situation is impossible. I
agreed to work with Cavanaugh in a hospital, with other
staff around to help buffer his angst. Staying here alone
with him is something else entirely. You coerced me into it.
And I want to come home. Today. Right now."

"What's she saying?" Lilah heard Thad ask.

"That she wants to come home."

"I was afraid of this. They're like fire and water. They
just don't mix, Elizabeth."

"But she's the best therapist we know. And Adam's the
best friend we've got. Here, you talk to her. She just gets
mad at me and thinks I'm trying to boss her."

Lilah rolled her eyes heavenward and impatiently
tapped her foot on the floor. As soon as she knew Thad had
the receiver back she said scathingly, "I'm not a child,
homesick and wanting to come back from camp, Thad.

Elizabeth's always been the big sister, but if anybody did the bossing, it was me. But she's right on target about my being mad. Coming to Maui wasn't part of the deal."

"It can't be all bad."

"I didn't say it was all bad. This house could be a sultan's palace. There's a cute, funny little man who is a cross between an angel and a slave. He thinks I'm wonderful and waits on me hand and foot." She sighed. "It's *him*. Casanova Cavanaugh. Treating a patient in his condition requires stamina and energy and boundless tolerance. And the bottom line is that I just can't tolerate Adam Cavanaugh."

"Put personal considerations aside, Lilah. The man needs you."

"It's not just *my* personal considerations. He's as dead set against my being here as I am. Believe me. He nearly had a stroke when I showed up yesterday. We simply can't stomach one another and never could."

"Give it a day or two more at least."

"But—"

"Has he shown any improvement?"

Compelled to tell the truth, she gave Thad a rundown of Adam's condition, including the muscle cramp and the improvement it signaled.

"Well, hell, I think that's great news!" he exclaimed. Lilah listened as he repeated it to Elizabeth. "So you've already made progress. Just hang in there. Adam'll come around. He'll get used to you."

But will I get used to him? To touching him? That was at the crux of her dilemma and the reason behind this phone call. Adam hadn't been the only one momentarily captivated by the sight of her very feminine hand juxtaposed to a very masculine part of his body. What that sight had done to her was far more terrifying than any temper tantrum he could throw.

"You can stick it out a few more days, can't you?" Elizabeth wheedled. Thad had passed the telephone receiver back to his wife.

Lilah sighed her surrender. "I guess I can. But start today to find a replacement. Check with the hospital. I'm sure my supervisor can give you a long list of competent therapists. I suggest a man. I think a man would work better with Cavanaugh." What woman, no matter how businesslike, could maintain a professional attitude toward that body?

"I'll see what I can do," Elizabeth told her, sounding unhappy about it.

"Today, Lizzie. Find someone to take my place."

"It won't be easy."

"Try."

"I will."

"*Try!*"

"*I will!*"

"I mean it, Elizabeth. What good will it do for me to get Cavanaugh to walk again, only to have him spend the rest of his life in prison for murdering me? I'm glad you think that's funny!"

Angered by her sister's spurt of laughter, she slammed

the receiver down. She hadn't even asked Elizabeth how she was feeling, but if she could laugh that hard, she must be feeling wonderful.

Lilah's professional integrity would be jeopardized if she deserted Adam in his present condition. Hopefully within a few days, though, she could leave and someone else would take over his physical therapy. In the meantime she would go through the motions as expertly as she knew how, but with as much detachment as she could maintain.

In that pragmatic frame of mind, she reentered Adam's bedroom. "Good. You ate all your breakfast." She removed the bed tray.

"What'd the doctor say?"

"The doctor?"

"Didn't you call the doctor?"

"Oh, uh, he wasn't in yet."

"He gets there early every morning."

"Then I guess he was making rounds."

"He said something you don't want to tell me, didn't he?" Adam asked suspiciously. "He told you not to get excited about the muscle cramp, that it didn't signify anything, right?"

Putting her hands on her hips she faced him. "God, you're paranoid."

"Then why don't you tell me what he said?"

"If you must know, I didn't talk to the doctor at all. I called Elizabeth and Thad."

"What for?"

"To quit." When Adam showed surprise, she demanded, "Well, isn't that what you want?"

"Yeah, sure, only—"

"Well?"

"You don't strike me as a quitter."

"I'm not. Usually. But our dislike for each other is so strong I'm afraid it will hamper your progress."

"Aren't you professional enough to put personal considerations aside?"

That was the second time in the space of a half hour that she'd heard those words. This time they were coming from Adam Cavanaugh in the form of a dare. His head was arrogantly tilted to one side, a nonverbal challenge in itself.

Turbulent blue eyes narrowed on him. "Damn right I am. Are you man enough to take the therapy without slinging personal insults at me?"

"Damn right."

"No slurs. No complaining. No temper tantrums."

"Agreed."

"Sometimes you'll hurt like hell, but I won't let up."

"I can take the pain."

"How badly do you want to walk again?"

"Walking isn't the issue. I want to run and sail and ski and . . . and climb that damn Italian peak."

"Then we've got weeks, possibly months, of hard work cut out for us. You'll work and sweat harder than you ever have. Before we're finished, you'll push yourself to limits of endurance you didn't know you had."

"I'm ready."

Lilah carefully hid her smile. His attitude had taken a complete turnaround. At least she'd achieved that much. He was no longer sulking like a wounded ogre, snarling at everybody who invaded his miserable space.

"What's first?" he asked, his eyes eager.

"A bath."

"Huh?"

"A bath. You stink, Mr. Cavanaugh."

FOUR

*H*E FOLDED HIS ARMS ACROSS HIS CHEST AND hunched his shoulders defensively. "I can't take a bath."

"Not in a tub, no. But I can give you one in bed."

She wheeled the hospital cart close to his bed. Taking a large washbowl from it, she disappeared into his bathroom to fill it with warm water.

"Pete can bathe me," Adam called to her.

"It's not Pete's job."

"It is if I say it is."

"I thought we had an agreement that you wouldn't complain," she said, huffing with exertion as she carried the filled bowl back to the cart.

"I didn't know our agreement included bed baths."

"It does. You should have read the fine print."

"A grown man being bathed in bed. It's humiliating."

"Not as humiliating as having BO."

With an assumed air of nonchalance she began to place towels under his body. He was capable of moving his torso to one side while she spread towels beneath it, but she had to roll his hips up in order to slide the towels beneath them and his legs.

To cover the awkwardness of the situation she asked, "Do you prefer a particular soap?"

"In the bathroom," he muttered.

She found a bar of soap in his shower. It was scented with an expensive, imported men's fragrance. "Very nice," she told him, sniffing at the bar. "Distinctive without being cloying."

"Glad you approve," was his sarcastic reply.

"Do you wear the cologne too?"

"Always."

"Then as soon as you shave you can put some cologne on."

"Shave?"

"Unless you'd rather I—"

"I can shave myself," he snapped.

"Then one might wonder why you haven't." She flashed him an insincere, sugary smile. "Or are you planning to grow that scraggly shadow into a full beard?"

He lapsed into a sullen silence as she folded back one side of the sheet and with efficient motions, dampened the washcloth and rubbed the soap into it until she had worked up a lather. She washed his foot first. As she was sponging his toes, she said, "Tickle?"

"Very funny."

"Come on, Cavanaugh, don't be such a sourpuss."

"Paralysis is something to laugh about?"

She frowned at him. "Laughter can't hurt. It might help. Are your toes normally ticklish?"

He turned his head and looked at her in a different way. His eyes gave her an insinuating once-over that was so hot it would have wilted the petals of the hibiscus on her chest had it been real. "Once I'm back to normal, maybe you can find out," he drawled in a sexy voice.

"I won't be giving you bed baths then."

"You wouldn't necessarily have to be giving me a bed bath. You could be doing something else to my toes."

"Like what?"

He named several pastimes, all prurient.

The washcloth became still in her hands for several telling seconds before she dipped it into the bowl to rinse it out. She shot Adam, who was smiling a tomcat grin, a sour glance. "How depraved."

"And fun."

"This conversation is bordering on the lascivious, Mr. Cavanaugh. That violates our agreement too." She patted him dry, then covered that leg and circled the end of the bed to wash the other.

"How so?"

"I don't discuss my private life with patients."

"Don't want them getting excited, huh?"

"Exactly."

He studied her for several minutes as she routinely went about her work. "I can't understand how you and Elizabeth grew up to be so different."

"Most people recognize us as sisters right off."

"There's a family resemblance," he said musingly, "but there the similarity ends. You're as different as night and day."

"We're both blond and blue eyed."

"Yes, but she's a dainty and feminine and soft blonde. And you're—"

Lilah replaced the sheet and glanced up at him curiously. "I'm what?"

"A bold and audacious and aggressive blonde."

"So is Hulk Hogan. Thanks a lot." She raised his right arm and began sponging it with the soapy cloth, even washing the fuzzy hollow of his armpit.

"I didn't mean it as an insult."

"Oh, really?"

"No. Apparently quite a few men have found your flamboyance attractive."

"Now, I'm flamboyant," she muttered out of the side of her mouth like a comic stepping out of character to address the audience.

Adam laughed. "The first time I saw you, you had a feather hanging from your ear and were wearing tight black leather pants and knee-high boots. I call that a bit flamboyant."

"That's one of my favorite outfits," she said defensively. "However, on that particular day I was wearing it at a patient's request."

"A man?"

"Uh-huh. He'd been injured in a motorcycle race. I wore the outfit to cheer him up."

"Did you?"

"Did I what?"

"Cheer him up."

She glanced down into Adam's face and saw that his expression, as well as his tone of voice, had turned serious. "Yes, I did."

"Do you always go to such extremes to cheer up your male patients?" There was a trace of accusation in his voice. Lilah chose to ignore it.

"I give all my patients equal consideration," she answered evenly.

"Do you?" He stopped her hand by covering it with his own.

During their conversation she'd been mechanically doing her duty. She realized now that his nipples were erect, having been lightly abraded by the washcloth. The carpet of dark chest hair was damp and curly. His heart was beating strongly into her palm.

Just how long had this conversation been going on? How long had her hands been moving over his chest? And for whose benefit? His or her own?

His softly spoken question brought her to attention. She dragged her hand free and quickly swished the cloth in the basin of water and wrung it out. "Here, wash your ears and neck and . . . and anything else I didn't get around to. Use this towel to dry yourself. I'll give you some privacy while I change the water."

She pushed the cart away from his bed so fast that water sloshed over the rim of the basin. Her hands were trembling when she carried it into the bathroom to empty into the tub. She refilled it and cleared her throat loudly to let him know that she was on her way back into the bedroom.

He was withdrawing his hand from beneath the sheet. She didn't look him directly in the eye when she took the washcloth from him and dampened it with fresh water. "Now your back."

"My back's fine."

"You said you had bedsores."

"I lied to get your sympathy."

"You're lying now."

"You'll never know."

"Look, Ace," she said, impatiently shifting all her weight to one shapely hip and throwing the other off center, "those sores are not going to get any better until they're washed and I get some of this antiseptic ointment on them." She took a silver tube of cream from a drawer in the cart and wagged it in front of his face. "If I don't treat them now, they'll probably get infected."

"Okay, okay. Roll me over like a slug."

"Next time spare us both the argument."

Adam wasn't muscle-bound, but he had a tall, rangy,

athletic body. It cost them both some effort to roll him to his side. She whistled when she saw the oozing blisters on his back and buttocks.

"Thanks," he said dryly.

"That wasn't a wolf whistle, Cavanaugh. This is icky."

"Is that a medical term?"

"No, that's my own word to paraphrase putrid, disgusting, and ugly."

"Your bedside manner needs work."

"Your backside needs work. Feel free to scream."

He didn't scream, but he cursed fluidly as she swabbed the sores, then liberally applied the healing ointment. "It's your own fault," she told him after he had issued a particularly lurid stream of gutter words. "You should have let Pete turn you every so often. From now on use the trapeze to help you shift positions."

"I practiced this morning."

"Good boy. You get a gold star."

"Are you finished?" He shot her a dark, threatening look over his shoulder.

She gave him a broad wink. "Finished what? Treating the sores or admiring your cute little buns?"

"Lilah," he ground out.

She smacked his taut cheek at a place where it was clear of abrasions. "Relax. I didn't have rape in mind. Has your incision been giving you any discomfort?" She examined it, touching it gently, but could see no cause for concern.

"It itches now and then."

"You can feel that?"

"Yes."

"Good. I see no problems with the scar. Your future lovers will probably find it fascinating."

"I'm glad to hear it. Are we done?"

"No, I'm going to wash your back now. That should feel very nice."

If his deep sighs were any indication, it felt wonderful. "I guess all that moaning and groaning means you approve," she remarked several minutes later as she blotted his skin dry. "How about some lotion?" She rubbed a dab of lotion between her hands and began massaging it into his back.

"That feels great. A little to the . . . ah, there. Hmm."

"You sound orgasmic," she teased.

"Compared to how I've felt recently, I am."

Smiling, she applied more pressure to her fingertips and slid her hands down the supple contours of his back. No fat here. No superfluous tissue. He was as tight as a drum.

"Lilah?"

"Hmm?"

"Will I ever be again?"

Alert to the change in his inflection, she lifted her hands so that they were no longer in contact with his skin. "Be what?"

"Orgasmic."

"Depends on whom you take to bed." Her jocularity was as flat as a three-day-old soda.

Reaching behind him, Adam caught her hand and pulled it forward until her arm was draped over his shoulder and her hand was tucked against his throat. "Don't play games with me. I want to know the truth. Will I ever be able to enjoy a woman again? Will a woman ever be able to enjoy me?"

Lilah stared down at his head and the tousled black hair that covered it. He was gorgeous. What woman wouldn't enjoy just looking at him? His profile was perfect, his nose straight and long, his jaw angular and strong. The uneven growth of stubble didn't detract from his handsomeness; it only added another dimension to it.

But he didn't want to hear that he was handsome. That no longer mattered. She doubted any man on earth would swap his virility for classic good looks. She had been asked this question by every male patient who found himself in circumstances similar to Adam's. It was what they always wanted to know first. When it came down to this crucial question, it didn't matter how many material possessions the man had, or how much money he had, or how much prestige he had been awarded. He wanted to know if his manhood was intact, if he would be sexually functional.

Lilah answered as truthfully as she was able. "I don't know, Adam. It will depend on which vertebrae, if any, were damaged beyond repair. Your body underwent a tremendous trauma. It'll take time and a lot of hard work, but it's my educated guess that you'll eventually be as good as new."

She eased him over onto his back. Her compassionate smile faltered when it was met by eyes filled with doubt and suspicion.

"You're lying."

Taken off guard by his unfair accusation, she counterattacked. "I am not!"

"You've all been lying to me."

"If the doctors told you they don't know, they don't know."

"They know," he snarled. "But why'd they send you to break the bad news to me? Or did you volunteer? Did you see this as your golden opportunity once and for all to win this private war we've been waging since we met?"

"You must have landed on your head when you fell off that mountain." The scarlet hibiscus bloom on the front of her T-shirt trembled with indignation. "I told you that I didn't want to come here. I tried to get out of it this morning, but Elizabeth whined and begged until I agreed to stay with you until they can find a replacement, which can't be soon enough for me. In the meantime I'll carry out my duties, but I won't put up with your abuse or crazy delusions."

He aimed an index finger at the tip of her nose. "Just don't lie to me."

"I didn't."

"And don't mock me."

"I haven't mocked you." She gasped, mortified at the thought. "I would never maliciously tease someone in your condition."

"Maybe not in words, but in deeds."

"Deeds? What the hell are you talking about?"

"For starters, you could wear decent clothes in front of me instead of fanning around in shorts. You look like a beach bunny scouting out her next easy lay."

"*What?*"

"Ever heard of shoes? Most women wear them on their feet out of propriety and modesty. They don't go barefoot unless . . . unless they're asking for it."

Her eyes grew dangerously dark. "You sexist slime."

"And I thought nurses wore caps instead of letting their hair hang free."

"I'm not a nurse."

"That's for damn sure. What kind of ointment was that? Those sores on my tail are killing me!"

"I'm delighted to hear it. It couldn't happen to a nicer guy."

She stormed toward the door. He grabbed hold of the trapeze above his head and pulled himself into a sitting position. "Where are you going? Get back here. I'm not through with you."

Whirling around, Lilah shouted, "Well, I'm through with you. For the time being anyway. You'd better rest up, buster, because when I come back this afternoon, we're going to get your blistered butt out of that bed. Understand?

"Between now and then, I want you to shave. You smell a damned sight better, but you still look like a street thug. If you're not shaved when I come back, I'll do it myself."

Her eyes glinted with blue malevolence. "And the way I feel right now, I don't think you want me anywhere near your throat with a razor."

She slammed the door behind her.

Lilah stared down into the glass-filled dustpan that Pete had tried to hide from her. "He won't own a drinking glass if he keeps this up." Pete emptied the shards of glass in the compactor. "What's he doing now?" He pantomimed sleeping and Lilah nodded. "Good. He'll need that rest this afternoon. Did he shave?"

Pete's face split into a wide grin. "Yes, then . . ." He slapped his cheeks and chin.

Lilah laughed and said to herself, "Cologne. Vanity is a healthy sign."

As long as Adam was napping, she put on a swimsuit and went out to enjoy the pool. Pete served her lunch on the terrace. She was dozing in a chaise lounge when he trotted out and tapped her on the arm.

"Doctor come."

"Oh, I didn't expect him until later." She pulled on her cover-up and padded into the house, meeting the doctor in the foyer. "Hi, Bo. You're here early, aren't you? Or did I fall asleep?"

"I'm early. I apologize. Right after you called, someone canceled an afternoon appointment, so I decided to take an earlier plane. How is he?"

"Meaner than a junkyard dog," she replied with an abruptness that startled the doctor. "Well, you asked."

"I was referring to his physical condition."

She filled in the gaps, having given him a cursory report over the telephone earlier. "I thought you should know about the spasticity."

"It's definitely a good sign. I'll examine him now."

She accompanied him upstairs and pointed out the room. "I'll wait if you don't mind. The last time I was in Mr. Cavanaugh's room, we were swapping death threats."

The doctor laughed, but he was unsure whether or not she was joking. As soon as the door to Adam's bedroom closed behind him, Lilah went to her suite and showered. She was dressed and waiting with a pitcher of chilled pineapple juice when he came back downstairs.

"I think he's made astounding progress," the doctor said enthusiastically, accepting the glass of juice with a nod of thanks. "He was working out on the pulleys when I went in."

"This afternoon I plan to get him on the tilt table. From there we'll go to a chair. The sooner he's mobile, the better his attitude is going to get."

"Despite the improvements, I noticed that he's still belligerent."

"That's an understatement. You might as well know that I've asked to be replaced."

"Oh?"

"I'm not the right therapist for Mr. Cavanaugh. Our personalities are on a collision course. They keep getting in the way."

"Sometimes that's exactly the kind of spark the patient

needs. Antagonism can act as a stimulant. It prompts them to try harder."

"Yes, well, that's all fine, well, and good, but I refuse to be Mr. Cavanaugh's personal punching bag."

"You've been a punching bag for other patients. That goes with the nature of your profession. You knew before you accepted this job that Mr. Cavanaugh was likely to be obnoxious and recalcitrant."

"Well, he's certainly living up to my expectations. I can't get anywhere with him."

"On the contrary, from what I've seen, you've been the tonic he needed. Speaking for myself and the other doctors who have been consulted on his case, I hope you stay, Ms. Mason. It would be a shame for you to desert this patient when you're making such tremendous headway."

"Is this the classic guilt trip you're laying on me or what?"

He smiled as he consulted his wristwatch. "I've got to leave you with the thought. The plane is waiting at the airfield to take me back to Oahu." He headed for the door, where Pete was standing by to open it. "Oh, almost forgot," the doctor said, nodding down at a large canvas mailbag that had been propped against the wall, "here is some mail that was sent to the hospital for Mr. Cavanaugh."

"All that?" Lilah asked incredulously.

"Your patient is a very popular man, Ms. Mason. I'm certain you're aware of how vital an individual he is. Or was until this tragic accident. He approached everything he did with an exuberance that never flagged. It's no wonder he's somewhat crotchety, is it, now? Well, good-bye. Call me daily and at any time if there's a change."

"Thanks for nothing," she mumbled as she watched his retreating back. She felt every ounce of the guilt he'd put on her as she climbed the stairs, anxious to see for herself all this tremendous headway the doctor had referred to.

Indeed, Adam did look better than he had that morning, and more than a close shave was responsible. "Hi," she said with uncharacteristic timidity.

"Hi."

"I approve." She indicated his shaved face.

"I approve," he said, taking in her more modest attire— jeans and sneakers.

"Well, I thought about putting on my burnoose and veil, but frankly, Cavanaugh, it's hot and uncomfortable and the material itches. So if this'll do . . ."

He laughed. "You're crazy." Gradually his smile faded until it disappeared altogether. His expression was serious when he asked, "Did it hurt?"

"What?"

"My beard. When I kissed you. Did it hurt?"

The scarlet blossom across her breasts trembled again. But not with indignation. "It scraped a little, I guess. I, uh, I didn't really notice."

"Oh." They stared at each other for an uncomfortable amount of time. Finally he said, "Well, I'm sorry if it did."

"That's okay." Nervously she dried her palms on her jeans and groped for a graceful means of switching subjects. "You did a real snow job on the doctor. He went on and on about how much you'd improved. Did you show off and perform a trick you haven't shown me?"

"Come here." She moved closer to his bed. He peeled back the sheet. She was amused to find him wearing a pair of briefs and wondered how much effort it had taken Pete and him to get them on. "Take a look at that."

"Calvin Klein," she remarked with a bored yawn. "I'm not label conscious."

"Not my underwear. Look."

He pointed down at his femoral muscle. She saw it flex slightly. "Bravo." Smiling down at him and applauding, she noticed that his brow was beaded with sweat. Just that much movement had taxed him, but it was movement and she couldn't have been more pleased. "How about going through some exercises to relax you?"

"Fine."

"Don't agree so readily. We'll move into the hard part soon."

She worked on all his joints, then rolled his hips one way while rolling his shoulders in the opposite direction. He was in that position when she asked, "By the way, who's Lucretia?" His head snapped around. "Well, I certainly struck a nerve there, didn't I?"

"How do you know about Lucretia?"

"I don't. That's why I asked. The doctor brought over a canvas bag full of mail for you. I glanced inside and the first three envelopes I saw had a return address in Switzerland and the name Lucretia von something or other foreign embossed in the corner."

"She's just this woman I was seeing."

"*Seeing?*"

"You know what I mean," he said crossly.

"Oh, yeah, I know what you mean. Seeing equals sleeping with."

"What of it?"

"Nothing. It's simply that I didn't know anybody really named their kid Lucretia."

"I didn't know anybody really named their kid Lilah."

She had the grace to laugh. "You've got a point. Good thing it doesn't have a *De* in front of it."

He considered her face for a moment, especially her mouth. "I don't know. That might have suited you even better."

Heat washed through her, but she attributed it to getting too much sun out by the pool. Unlike Elizabeth, she had never blushed in her life. "Is your Lucretia related to Lucrezia Borgia?"

"No, but I think you are. Dammit, stop that." The words rushed out, tumbling over each other.

She was trying to bend his knee at a right angle and the limb was resisting the movement. She applied more pressure. He gnashed his teeth and made a hissing sound. "Does that hurt?"

"Hell, yes, it—" His gaze sprang to hers. "Is that good?"

"Yes, numskull. Let's work together to try to bend it. The day will come when you'll try to bend it and I'll work against you. That's when you'll really hate me."

"Make me walk, Lilah, and I'll love you."

For a moment their eyes locked. Lilah was the first to glance away. She made a joke out of it. "They all say that. How soon they forget when they're well."

She made several more attempts at bending both his knees. It cost them energy and sweat. Still, she didn't let up. Not until she and Pete had transferred him to the tilt table and he had stood upright on it for almost half an hour.

"You've been goldbricking, haven't you, Cavanaugh?"

He smiled, looking extremely proud of himself. "I was up to half an hour twice a day before I left the hospital."

"Then it was really stupid of you to leave."

"It didn't seem like much, standing against a table that was actually doing the standing for me."

"But it is much. Since you're so adept at it, I think we can move on to bigger and better things."

When he was stretched out full on his bed again, he drew in a breath of profound relief. "I'm always afraid I'm going to tip out of that thing. I'm glad it's over."

"Hardly over, Cavanaugh. Take five. Then we really go to work."

She crossed to the door and pulled it open with a flourish. Using the same theatrics, she disappeared for a second. When she returned, she was riding in a wheelchair.

FIVE

"*BEEP BEEP.*" *SHE MADE SEVERAL TRIPS* around the room before bringing the wheelchair to a stop at his bedside. Smiling up at him, she used a corny twang to say, "It comes loaded with options. Wire wheels, custom upholstery, power steering. Low mileage, too. Yessiree, you'd do well to put your money into this baby." Her audience wasn't amused. In fact, Adam's deep frown expressed intense dislike. "Would you rather see another model?"

"Get that damn thing out of my sight."

"*What?* I thought you'd be excited."

"I don't care what you thought. I won't humiliate myself by struggling to get out of bed, only to wind up in a chair I don't want to be in. The doctor says I'm making progress from here. That's good enough for me."

"Oh, I doubt that." She leapt from the chair and bore

down on him. "Are you reconciled to spending the rest of your life in bed?"

"If necessary."

She stubbornly shook her head. "Well, you might be ready to give up, but I'm not."

"What business is it of yours?"

"You're my patient."

"So?"

"So, until you can fight me off, you're at my mercy."

"What do you mean?"

Rather than answer him, she marched to the door and flung it open. "Pete! Get up here," she hollered in a most unladylike fashion. In a matter of seconds his tiny shoes were making slapping sounds on the stairs.

"Yes, Rirah?"

"Help me get Mr. Cavanaugh into the wheelchair. Then bring that van around to the front door."

"We go?"

"That's right. We go. And so does he." She hitched her head backward to indicate Adam.

His face was stony, his jaw indomitable. "I'm not going anywhere."

"Yeah, yeah, you've come here to die the way ancient Indians and elephants go into the mountains to await death. You'd like to lie here in your own self-pity and let those perfectly beautiful muscles in your legs shrivel." She jabbed him in the chest. "But I'm not going to let you."

"You can't force me to do anything I don't want to do."

"You're right, I can't. But before you make up your mind to quit, I want to show you something."

"I don't know what you plan to do, but you'll never pull it off."

"Oh, no?" She flashed him a dazzling smile that soon turned brittle and hard. "Watch me." She approached the bed. "Okay, Pete. I'll get his top. You take his feet."

Stepping behind Adam, she leaned him forward from the waist. Sliding her arms beneath his, she spanned his torso and locked her hands together in front of his chest.

He fought viciously, flailing his arms. "Save your strength, Cavanaugh. I've handled men who outweigh you by a hundred pounds."

"Let me go, you bitch." He tried to pry her fingers apart, but she squeezed them into fists.

"If you don't calm down, I'll restrain you," she warned. "I'll tie your arms down. Ready, Pete?"

"Damn you, no!" Adam roared as she hoisted his body over the edge of the bed and lowered him into the wheelchair. Pete, not wanting to be involved but realizing the necessity of it, followed Lilah's directions and placed Adam's feet on the footplates.

Adam immediately curled his fingers around the armrests of the chair and levered himself up. Lilah knew that trick. Before he succeeded in launching himself up and out, she stepped in front of him.

"Don't even try it. If you do, I'll tie you in there, I swear. We're going out for a drive. You either go with dignity or without. It's up to you."

His dark eyes drilled into hers with a hatred that was as palpable as it was normal at this stage in his therapy. Lilah tried her best to ignore and not reciprocate it. But at the moment she felt like slapping him. "Pete, go get the van."

He scuttled out thankfully. Lilah stepped behind the wheelchair, released the brake, and pushed it forward. They had no difficulty getting to the elevator, which she had been delighted to discover earlier in the day. But because of Adam's height and weight, she had trouble lifting the wheels of the chair over the door facings. They reached the front of the house just as Pete was bringing the specially equipped van around. She rolled the chair into place and locked it down.

"Aren't you even curious as to where we're going?" she asked, looking into Adam's hostile face as the hydraulic lift raised the wheelchair into the van.

What he did was universally accepted as the ultimate show of contempt.

"Guess that answers my question." She secured the wheelchair inside the van and climbed in herself. "For your information, Dr. Arno made arrangements for the van. You're free to use it as long as it's necessary. You might want to send him a thank-you note."

Adam merely turned his head aside and stared disinterestedly through the window. Pete, sitting on a cushion because of his short stature, put the van in gear. Lilah gave him directions as he drove, but if Adam guessed where she was taking him, he gave no indication of it.

Only when Pete drove through the gates of the institution did Adam show any emotion or interest. When he read the name on the discreet sign, he whipped his head around and silently demanded an explanation from her.

"That's right, Adam. This is a rehab center for para- and quadriplegics. If you weren't so damned rich and able to afford private care, this is where you might be. Drive slowly, Pete. I want him to see this."

"Look over there," she said, pointing through the windshield. "There are two teams of men playing basketball. I'm sure none of them chose to be in a wheelchair. They'd rather be running up and down the court, but at least they're laughing, having a good time, making the best of a tragic situation.

"Stop a moment, Pete." Pete did as she asked. "There's the swimming pool, Adam. Look at all those children. They're behaving very much like ordinary children do in a swimming pool. Except they're not ordinary. They're very special." Her eyes glazed with tears. "Special because it's not easy for them to even get to a pool, much less swim in one. They can't run off a diving board and jump in. They can't do a cannonball or go the length of the pool underwater."

Too emotional to say anything more, she signaled Pete forward again. When he stopped at a crosswalk, they watched and waited while a nurse wheeled her paraplegic charge across the street. The young patient was smiling at something the nurse had said.

"Take a good look at her, Adam. You are very much alike. But there are two major differences. She's smiling, not sulking. And her paralysis is permanent." Lilah spread her arms wide to encompass the entire compound. "That's right. Everybody here will stay in a wheelchair for life. And they're grateful for even that much mobility."

She furiously swiped at the tears that were rolling down her cheeks. "How dare you . . . how *dare* you behave with such unconscionable selfishness when you have an excellent chance of walking again, of living a normal life, and they don't." She shuddered. Staring Adam down, she said tightly, "Take us home, Pete."

It was a long, silent ride home.

The following morning she waited until she knew Adam had eaten breakfast and shaved before going into his room. Upon their return the evening before she had got him back into bed, then left him without a word. Though it had been a breach of professional ethics, she'd had no second thoughts about taking him to the rehab center. He had deserved the shock treatment. She shouldn't have left him alone through the night either, but she had. She had been afraid that if she touched Adam Cavanaugh at all, it would be to wrap her hands around his throat and strangle him.

Now she paused on the threshold of his bedroom, not knowing whether she would have to dodge a flying missile or not. But when he saw her, instead of hurling the coffee mug he was drinking from, he merely placed it on the nightstand. "Good morning."

"Good morning," she replied. "Sleep well?"

"Around three this morning I had some cramps."

"I'm sorry. You should have called me."

He shrugged. "I used the trapeze to change position. They went away."

"Were they bad?"

"Like a charley horse."

"In your calves?"

"Mostly the backs of my thighs."

"You should have taken a pain pill."

"I survived without one." He glanced down at the tent that his toes poked in the sheet. Wisely, she opted to remain silent and let him direct the conversation. After a brief silence he looked up and asked, "Why didn't you kick my butt yesterday?"

"When it was covered with decubitus ulcers? You must think I'm a monster."

One corner of his lip tilted up into a rueful smile, but his eyes were anything but jovial. "I've been acting like a real jerk."

"You won't get an argument from me."

"How'd . . ." He paused to clear his throat. "How'd you know about that rehabilitation center?"

"Dr. Arno told me about it. He suggested that when I wasn't needed here, I might think of spending some time there. Volunteers are in short supply. They always need more than they've got."

"I've owned this house for years. I never knew that hospital was there," he said as he absently turned his eyes toward the window.

Lilah detected a bad case of melancholia coming on.

Taking him to the rehab center had gotten her point across, but she didn't want to overshoot her mark. The last thing he needed to be was depressed.

"That was a pretty rotten surprise I pulled on you yesterday," she told him. "So if you'll forgive me that, I'll forgive you for acting like a jerk, okay? Besides, if you hadn't acted like a jerk I would have thought you were abnormal. All patients, particularly young, athletic men, go through that jerky stage first."

"Because they're afraid they'll never get laid again."

"First and foremost," she said, laughing.

"Fairly strong basis for concern, wouldn't you agree?"

"Yes," she answered hesitantly, "but you don't have to worry about that today. Today you have to worry about getting into the wheelchair by yourself."

"It'll never work," he said, shaking his head dejectedly. "I'll never be able to do that."

"Sure you will. You'll be zipping around here in no time. Luckily the builder of this house thought to install an elevator."

"How did you know about that anyway? The elevator is supposed to be a secret. Did Pete tell you?"

"No, I discovered it while I was snooping around."

"What else did you discover?"

"Your stock of brandy and your collection of porno flicks."

"Drink any brandy?"

"An inch or two."

"Good?"

"Delicious."

"Watch any flicks?"

"Repugnant, revolting, and repulsive."

"That's redundant."

"But arresting and articulate alliteration."

Wincing, he booed her. "How many movies did you watch before deciding they were revolting, repulsive, and so on?"

"Four." He laughed. Defensively she said, "Well, I had to pass the time somehow. I couldn't sleep last night."

"Why?"

"Because I knew my patient was going to distract me this morning to keep from working on getting himself out of bed. I was trying to devise a means of avoiding that."

"Have any luck?"

"Obviously not."

They laughed together, and it came as a surprise to each of them what a good time they were having with the verbal sparring.

Lilah drew herself up to a more professional posture. "Guess I'll just have to be a slave driver." He groaned. "Come on now, sit up as far as you can."

"Even when I'm in the wheelchair, I won't be able to go anywhere."

"Pete's downstairs with a carpenter now. He's installing temporary ramps over all the door facings. You'll be able to move through the entire house."

"Whoopee," he said drolly.

"Do you want to do this or not?" Facing him with her

hands on her hips, the beer advertisement on her T-shirt was stretched tight across her breasts.

Adam was quick to appreciate the view. "I love it when you get rowdy."

"This is nothing. You ought to see me when I get hot."

His eyes widened marginally with surprise, then narrowed a degree as he said softly, "I'd like that."

"You certainly would," she cooed, giving him a promising smile, which she hastily reversed. "But not today."

"Then you should be more careful."

"Careful?"

"I can see the outline of your nipples."

Lilah's stomach did a series of flip-flops, but she tried to appear unaffected. "Would looking at them help get you out of bed?"

"It might. Let's give it a try."

He reached for the hem of her T-shirt. She swatted his hand aside. "Sorry, that's not on this morning's agenda."

The men who flirted with Lilah ranged from construction workers on the city streets to surgeons in the corridors of the hospital. No shrinking violet, she could hold her own with any of them. She rarely got flustered. This time she came close.

Male patients often used vulgarity just to get a shocked reaction out of the women on the hospital staff. Like children, they wanted to see how far they could go before being reprimanded.

But Adam didn't look like a child. He didn't sound like a child. He didn't even have the mischievous gleam in his eye that most patients did when trying to goad her. He looked and sounded deadly serious. For a forbidden instant Lilah was tempted to take his hand and draw it to her breast. She had to shake her blond head in order to clear it of the tempting thought.

"Can we get down to business now?" she asked authoritatively.

"Sure."

His grin told her his mind was still on pleasure, not business, but she would soon fix that. "How are your biceps?"

"They're fine. Why?"

"Enjoy them. By this time tomorrow night they'll be sore. You'll have to support yourself on them to lift yourself off the edge of the bed and into the chair."

He nodded brusquely. "Got it."

"Wait a minute, Ace." Laughing, she placed her hands on his shoulders and eased him back against the pillows. "There's a technique to this."

"So show me," he demanded in the imperious tone of voice that had galvanized hotel managers into action and reduced sloppy chambermaids to tears.

It took almost half an hour to get him into the chair. By the end of it they were both exhausted and their breathing was labored. "I'm not sure it's worth the effort." He looked up at her. A lock of hair had fallen over his perspiring brow.

Reflexively Lilah reached toward him and brushed it back into place. "It will be, I promise. This is just the first time. Remember the first time you tried to snow ski? Bet you said, 'I'm not sure it's worth the effort.' "

He nodded with chagrin. "I think I was into the third day of instruction before I stopped saying that. The only sport that was worth the effort the first time I did it was sex. It took me an hour and a half to persuade Aurielle Davenport to go all the way."

"I'm surprised it didn't take you longer than that. She sounds like a real snob who would hold out forever."

"Pretty snobby. But at the time I wasn't thinking of her character."

"She was a sex object for your adolescent lust."

He laughed. "Guilty. But Aurielle wasn't thinking about my character either."

"So when did this momentous occasion occur?"

"During Thanksgiving break my junior year in high school."

"And sex has remained a sport to you ever since?"

He glanced up at her over his shoulder. "Sure. Isn't that what it is to you?"

"Sure." Their gazes locked. It was a long time before Lilah said, "Hey, as long as you're in that thing, want to go for a ride?"

"Okay." He settled back against the seat. When she made no move to propel him forward, he looked up at her expectantly. "Well?"

"If you think I'm going to spend my spare time chauffeuring you around, Mr. Cavanaugh, you've got another think coming."

"For a thousand bucks a day you should be willing to sprout wings and fly if I tell you to."

"You checked?"

"Damn right."

She was pleased that he had taken enough interest in his business affairs to call the mainland and check on her fee. But she frowned down at him as though perturbed. "I'm a free agent, not one of your flunkies whose only aim in life is to make the big, bad boss happy." Stubbornly, she folded her arms over her middle.

When it became obvious that she wasn't going to relent, he growled, "How do you run this damn thing?"

"Thought you'd never ask," she said cheerfully.

They practiced on the gallery. Soon he was accustomed to operating the wheelchair by himself. "This isn't so bad," he said with a broad smile. "I've seen guys, you know, who *run* marathons in wheelchairs, popping wheelies in these things."

"Please, don't try that yet. Give it a day or two at least," she said teasingly. "Thad does wheelies on his motorcycle sometimes. The kids love it. Elizabeth goes berserk."

"Thad has a bike?"

"Goes against type, doesn't it?"

"He's a great guy."

"Yes, he is. I'm so glad he found my sister. Or vice versa."

"They seem to be very happy together."

"They're positively gaga and goo-goo. It gets disgusting sometimes. But that's what Elizabeth wants and needs, someone to love, someone who loves her devotedly. Thad was a perfect choice." She gave Adam a sidelong glance. "Better than you."

"*Me?*"

"For a while there I thought you were courting my sister. I even encouraged her to fool around a little before making up her mind between the two of you."

"I was courting her *professionally.*"

"I recall an evening when you showed up at her door with a bouquet of roses, looking for all the world like a beau."

"The night you burned the cookies. Elizabeth told me about it later," he said by way of explanation when her mouth dropped open in surprise. "The evening got off to an inauspicious beginning. Remember Thad and I had brought her identical bouquets."

"I remember laughing myself sick over Matt's blurting that out. Wonder what would have happened if Thad hadn't been there, glowering dire threats at you?"

"Between Elizabeth and me, you mean? Nothing. Nothing except what did, that is. We'd still be business partners, but nothing else. Don't get me wrong, Elizabeth is a beautiful woman. I have always enjoyed her company. But I knew what she wanted and needed. I also knew I wasn't it."

"A husband, a father for her kids. That scene isn't for you, huh?"

"No more than it is for you."

"Love and sex are recreational."

"Right," he answered shortly, then gave her a long, steady gaze. "Right?"

"Oh, right. Absolutely. Well, here we are," she said as she took over control of the chair and guided it to a halt beside his bed. "Now, to get you back into bed we simply reverse the procedure."

He groaned loudly. "You mean we gotta go through that *again?*"

SIX

*T*HEY STILL FOUGHT LIKE CATS AND DOGS, BUT their relationship drastically improved.

He still cursed her and accused her of being a heartless bitch who, out of pure meanness, pushed him beyond his threshold of pain and endurance.

She still cursed him and accused him of being a gutless rich kid who, for the first time in his charmed life, was experiencing hardship.

He said she couldn't handle patients worth a damn.

She said he couldn't handle adversity worth a damn.

He said she taunted him unmercifully.

She said he whined incessantly.

And so it went. But things were definitely better.

He came to trust her just a little. He began to listen when she told him that he wasn't trying hard enough and should put more concentration into it. And he listened

when she advised that he was trying too hard and needed
to rest awhile.

"Didn't I tell you so?" She was standing at the foot of
his bed, giving therapy to his ankle.

"I'm still not ready to tap dance."

"But you've got sensation."

"You stuck a straight pin into my big toe!"

"But you've got sensation." She stopped turning his
foot and looked up toward the head of his bed, demanding
that he agree.

"I've got sensation." The admission was grumbled, but
he couldn't hide his pleased smile.

"In only two and a half weeks." She whistled. "You've
come a long way, baby. I'm calling Honolulu today and
ordering a set of parallel bars. You'll soon be able to stand
between them."

His smile collapsed. "I'll never be able to do that."

"That's what you said about the wheelchair. Will you
lighten up?"

"Will you?" He grunted with pain as she bent his knee
back toward his chest.

"Not until you're walking."

"If you keep wearing those shorts, I'll soon be running.
I'll be chasing you."

"Promises, promises."

"I thought I told you to dress more modestly."

"This is Hawaii, Cavanaugh. Everybody goes casual, or
haven't you heard? I'm going to resist the movement now.
Push against my hand. That's it. A little harder. Good."

"Ah, God," he gasped through clenched teeth. He followed her instructions, which took him through a routine to stretch his calf muscle. "The backs of your legs are sunburned," he observed as he put forth even greater effort.

"You noticed?"

"How could I help it? You flash them by me every chance you get. Think those legs of yours are long enough? They must start in your armpits. But how'd I get off on that? What were we talking about?"

"Why my legs were sunburned. Okay, Adam, let up a bit, then try it again. Come on now, no ugly faces. One more time." She picked up the asinine conversation in order to keep his mind off his discomfort. "My legs are sunburned because I fell asleep beside the pool yesterday afternoon."

"Is that what you're being paid an exorbitant amount of money to do? To nap beside my swimming pool?"

"Of course not!" After a strategic pause, she added, "I went swimming too." He gave her a baleful look and pressed his foot against the palm of her hand. "Good, Adam, good. Once more."

"You said that was the last one."

"I lied."

"You heartless bitch."

"You gutless preppy."

Things were swell.

*　　*　　*

"Elizabeth, drat her, had a perfect arch that our teacher oohed and aahed over. Her dainty foot was always on exhibit, something the rest of us in the class should aspire to. She was a perfect little ballerina with perfect form. She got all the solo roles in the recitals. When she danced, the teacher got tears in her eyes. I was always stuck on the back row. I was swaybacked and looked like a goose trying to dance *Swan Lake*. The teacher cried when I performed, too, but it wasn't quite the same."

Adam's rumble of laughter vibrated through Lilah's fingertips as she massaged his back. He was relaxed; she was glad. She had really put him through his paces that morning and his muscles were quivering with fatigue.

"When we got to junior high, Mother put us in ballroom dancing. Elizabeth glided through as gracefully as Ginger Rogers. I was head and shoulders taller than all the boys in the class. I spilled punch on my dress at the first dance. I was such a disaster at being a lady, I stopped trying and became the class clown instead. The teacher telephoned Mother and offered her her money back if she would take me out of the class. 'Disruptive element' was the diplomatic phrase I think she used."

"I'll bet you were relieved you didn't have to go back."

Drawing her face into a frown, she didn't answer for a moment. "Not really. It amounted to just one more failure."

Adam raised his head off the mat table high enough to look back at her. "Because you didn't hack it in ballroom dancing?"

"Well, that and about six million other endeavors. Elizabeth made straight A's. I was a solid B student. But that seemed such a tepid second place, so I deliberately started making C's. Just high enough to pass. My sister was an exemplary pupil, every teacher's pet, so I became the scourge of teachers throughout the system. Whatever Elizabeth was, I wanted to be the opposite."

"You resent her that much?"

"I don't resent her at all. I love and adore her. It's simply that I recognized early on that I couldn't ever be like her, so I wanted to become radically different. Otherwise I was afraid I'd fade into the woodwork and nobody would ever see me."

"I seriously doubt you'd ever go unseen," he said with a chuckle.

"Roll over. Come on, spare me the groan. You can do it."

He did, using his arm muscles and those in his hips and thighs that he had gradually regained the use of. He shifted himself from table to wheelchair, then from wheelchair to bed with very little assistance.

"There. That's it for now," she told him once he was reclining against the pillows. "Need anything before I go?"

"Yeah. There *is* something I could use." Smiling guilelessly, he told her.

In spite of her own pungent vocabulary and ribald wit, she blushed. "I don't do that."

"Ever?"

"Not to patients."

"You offered by saying 'anything.' "

"I had in mind fetching you some fruit juice, a magazine, the TV remote control."

"In that case, no thanks."

"Okay, see you later." She turned to go.

"What's your hurry? Where are you going?"

"Shopping."

"What for?"

"I need some things."

"What things?"

"Personal things."

"Like what?"

"How indelicate! Now, good-bye. The afternoon is getting away."

"Are you taking the van?"

"My rental car."

"Take the van. I'll ride along with you."

Lilah shook her head. "I've got several stops to make. You'd get tired before I was ready to come back."

"No, I wouldn't."

"Yes, you would. Besides, when I finish running errands, I thought I'd spend an hour or two helping out at the rehab center."

"What about me?"

"What about you?"

"How long will you be gone?"

"I don't know, Adam," she said with mounting exasperation. "What difference does it make?"

"I'll tell you what difference it makes," he said angrily.

"I'm paying you a thousand bucks a day to take care of me."

"But I get time off for good behavior, don't I?"

"When has your behavior ever been good?"

"I'm leaving," she said in a singsong voice.

"You can't," he called after her. "I might need you here."

"Pete will be here if you need anything. See ya."

"Lilah?"

"*What?*" She turned back toward the bed again. Her expression was indulgent, but impatient.

"Don't rush off." He had switched tactics. No longer angry, he was wheedling. "Pete's available, but he doesn't sit down and talk to me."

"You and I have been talking all morning. I've run out of things to say."

"We'll play Trivial Pursuit."

"We always fight when we play."

"We'll play poker."

"No fair. You always win."

"Strip poker?"

"No fair. I'd win. You're already down to your skivvies."

"So strip down to yours and we'll start even." She gave him a dirty look. Laughing, he relented. "Okay, if strip poker is out, we could watch a movie on the VCR."

"We've watched all of them. Twice."

"Not the skin flicks."

"I pass."

"Not too prudish, are you?"

"Not in the mood."

"They'll put you in the mood, I promise."

She shifted her stance impatiently. "You know what I mean."

He pulled his lower lip through his teeth several times. "Come on, Lilah, don't run out on me. I'm bored."

"But I'm not a social director. Good-bye, Adam," she said firmly, and left before he could say anything more.

Had she stayed longer, he might have succeeded in changing her mind. Lately she was staying in his room more than necessary. Each time she left, she found it a little harder to go.

"How's the water?"

"Feels terrific. Want to get in?"

"No, not tonight."

Lilah emerged from the pool and reached for a beach towel. As she dried off, she was conscious of Adam's eyes on her. For that very reason, she usually used the pool when he was upstairs resting.

Tonight, however, he had insisted on sitting outside longer than usual after dinner. The moon was up. It was a gorgeous night. After holding out as long as she could, hoping Adam would retire to his room, Lilah had yielded to the pool's temptation, dropped her cover-up, and dived in to swim several laps.

"Any of that mail interesting?" she asked as she rubbed her wet hair with a corner of the towel.

"Not really. Just plentiful. I'll never get finished sorting it all, much less answering it."

"Must be tough to be loved by thousands," she remarked tongue-in-cheek. "What do the piles represent?"

He had formed three hills of correspondence on the patio table in front of him. "The good, the bad, and the ugly," he said, enumerating each pile.

Lilah leaned out of her chaise and dug into the "ugly" pile, coming up with an envelope. She held it up closer to the flaming torch that was burning from the metal pole cemented in the flower bed behind her. "Thad and Elizabeth Randolph," she said, reading the return address on the envelope.

"Oops, they got in the wrong pile."

"I don't think you're paying much attention to that sorting method of yours." Uncaring that the letter had been addressed to him, she worked her finger into the slit of the envelope.

"I wasn't paying attention. I was watching you swim." Lilah's finger got stuck. She looked up at Adam. "Why don't you skinny-dip?"

"Why don't you behave?" she asked, slightly breathless.

"It would be a helluva sight."

"Thanks."

"You're welcome." They stared at each other for a long moment. Finally breaking the gaze, Adam nodded at the forgotten envelope in her hand. "What do the Randolphs have to say?"

She ripped open the envelope and took out the letter. Her eyes scanned it, though after that brief but potent exchange with Adam, it took awhile for her sister's words to sink in.

"They hope you're doing well and that I'm not causing you too much grief." He grunted with amusement. "She failed to ask how I'm doing. Thanks a lot, Lizzie," Lilah muttered. "It says here that Megan got upset when her softball team lost in the city playoffs."

"Poor baby. How's Matt?"

"Uh-oh. He had to spend an entire day in his room for teaching his best friend a nasty word."

"He must have picked it up from his Aunt Lilah."

She threw her wet towel at Adam's head. "Matt's my buddy. He thinks I'm terrific."

"How is Elizabeth feeling?"

Lilah read on. "She says she feels great. Thad is her main pain. 'He's acting more absurd as my due date draws closer.' Oh, my gosh, listen to this. He bought new tires for both their cars on the outside chance they'd have a flat on the way to the hospital." Lilah made a scoffing sound. "The guy's gone bonkers over this kid."

Adam laughed, but his voice sounded reflective when he said, "Must be nice though."

"What?" Lilah asked, replacing the letter in the envelope.

"Knowing you'd created another human life." When he turned his head and looked at her, his eyes caught the wavering torchlight.

"Oh, that. Well, I guess it is a nice feeling. If you're into that."

"Yeah, if you're into that."

They were silent for a moment. Lilah spoke first. "About these letters, can I help? I wouldn't mind forging a few cursory responses for you. Something to the effect of, 'Thanks for your concern, period. Sincerely, comma. Adam Cavanaugh.'"

"I've got offices of people who can do that. I'll have Pete box them all up and send them to the corporate headquarters."

"Even the personal notes?" She was indirectly referring to the scores of letters he had received from Lucretia. They had been set aside and read but as far as she knew, had gone unanswered.

"I guess I should attend to those, it's just—" He sighed deeply. "I feel detached. You know?" He looked at her for confirmation. She nodded her head, even though she wasn't sure what he was leading up to.

"I missed the gala grand opening of the Hotel Cavanaugh in Zurich last week. Ordinarily I would have been there, running the show, finalizing details, checking this and that, personally making sure that everything went well and according to schedule. But"—he paused and made a negligent gesture—"I don't really think I missed much."

"You've got more on your mind. There's much more at stake now than the opening of a new hotel. The accident changed your perspective on things. You've got a different set of priorities."

"I guess that's it. Or maybe I'm just tired. Since my father died and I launched out on my own, I've been driven to have more, make more, do more."

"Overachieve."

"Yes."

Lilah knew his story through Elizabeth. Adam had inherited a small chain of mediocre motels from his father. He had sold them as soon as the will was probated. With the profit he had built a first-class hotel that had enjoyed immediate success. That first hotel had grown into a chain of eighteen. No matter where in the world it was located, a Hotel Cavanaugh stood for excellence in quality and service.

Adam had had a head start, granted, inheriting sizable legacies from both his parents, but it could be said truthfully that he was a self-made millionaire.

"I was bored with my life even before my accident," he admitted to Lilah now. "That sounds insensitive, doesn't it?"

"A little," she told him with a soft smile. "You're to be envied for all you have."

"I realize that. The boredom wasn't something I was proud of. Why was I bored?"

"You had reached all your goals and had run out of challenges. That's why you invented them, like climbing that mountain."

He turned introspective. "It seems a lifetime ago when Pierre, Alex, and I planned that climb. It's hard for me to envision myself involved in things like that again. I've been invited to spend a month next spring with friends on a yacht in the Mediterranean. I never take that long a vacation from work, but even if I did, the prospect doesn't sound appealing. I feel so distant from it all—the beautiful people, fast cars, rich food, fancy boats. The hotels. The women." He turned his head and fixed a hard stare on Lilah.

She swallowed with difficulty. "That'll pass. You feel detached and distant because you are. Out of necessity your focus has to be on getting back to normal. Once you are, you'll get into the swing again."

"I'm not sure."

"Oh, yes," she said. "That drive to overachieve is in your character. The passion to succeed is in your genes just like your dark eyes. Elizabeth says your energy is so boundless you always leave her feeling breathless. She describes you as being constantly in motion. That'll come back."

"But I'll never be the same. I don't mean physically," he said when he saw she was about to disagree. "I'll never think the same about life, the human condition."

"No, Adam, you'll never be the same. At some time in the distant future you might be very glad this happened to you." She left the lounger and moved toward his wheelchair, pulling it away from the table. "Tell you the truth, Ace," she said in a much lighter tone, "all this philosophy is wearing me down. Why don't we call it a night, huh?"

"I'm not tired."

"Don't argue— Adam! What are you doing?"

With a strength and agility that amazed her, he reached behind the chair, grabbed her hand, and dragged her around to the front of it. She landed hard in his lap. He encircled her with his arms and clasped his hands together, trapping her.

"What am I doing?" he repeated playfully. "Don't you recognize it? I'm putting the make on you."

His words made her heart flutter, but she looked at him sternly. "You could have hurt yourself. Such impulsiveness could be harmful."

"I'm not acting on impulse. I've been thinking about this for days."

"About what?"

He lowered his mouth to hers and kissed her. He knew how to kiss. From Aurielle Davenport to Lucretia von what's her name, he had no doubt had plenty of practice kissing. His mouth applied a slight suction to hers that sealed them together. His tongue was active but not invasive. It penetrated slowly and deliciously.

Echoing the hungry sounds that vibrated in his throat, Lilah kissed him back. Then, realizing that she shouldn't be, she angled her head back and away. "No, Adam."

"Yes." His searching lips found her neck arched and wanting.

"This isn't part of the therapy program."

"It's part of *my* program." His whisper conveyed the urgency with which he reached around her and unfastened the bra of her bikini. It dropped into her lap. Lowering his head, he rubbed his cheek against her breasts and nuzzled the deep cleavage between them with his nose and lips.

Lilah made a whimpering sound that could have meant pleasure, regret, or guilt. Or any combination thereof. "Adam, stop, please. You don't know what you're doing."

"The hell I don't." He took a gentle lovebite out of the soft fullness of her breast, then kissed the spot, pressing his lips into her flesh.

"You just want me because I'm here."

"I just want you."

"Because you're dependent on me."

"Because you're sexy as hell."

"You kissed me before."

"That wasn't a kiss. That was an insult."

"And this follows. It fits right into the pattern. First the fury, then the infatuation. You're mistaking dependency for desire."

"I've never mistaken desire, Lilah." As they formed the words, his lips tantalizingly brushed her nipple, bringing it to a peak.

She moaned when his tongue began to feather it rapidly. "Don't, don't."

He didn't give credence to her feeble plea, but drew the stiff crest between his lips and sucked it lightly. "You're sweet, Lilah," he murmured while moving his mouth to her other breast. "Do you taste this sweet all over?"

She embedded her fingers in his hair, intending to lift his head away from her. But she couldn't bring herself to.

His warm, wet mouth was giving her pleasure, the likes of which she had never felt before. Heat swirled through her breasts, between her thighs, creating an exquisite, feverish ache. "This is wrong, Adam, a big mistake."

"Then why are you letting me do it?" He raised his head and looked deeply into her troubled eyes.

"I don't know," she answered, her voice tinged with desperation and confusion. "I don't know."

He whisked a kiss across her lips. "Because you want to be kissed as much as I want to kiss you. Don't lie about it. I won't believe you."

As his mouth captured hers again, his hands closed over her breasts. He kneaded them gently while his tongue mated with hers. His thumbs indolently stroked her nipples, which were still damp from his kisses.

Weakly, Lilah laid her hands on his shoulders. He wasn't wearing a shirt. His skin, which she knew intimately by touch alone, was smooth and warm. She longed to fling her arms around his neck and draw the hairy warmth of his chest against her bare skin, but she resisted the temptation.

Her mind was muzzy with passion, but clear enough to realize that she was violating a staunch professional creed without quite knowing how it had come about or at what point she had lost control of the situation. It was imperative that she get it back.

She pushed against his shoulders at the same time she stood up. Her bikini bra fell to the terrace. She bent to retrieve it, then turned her back and replaced it. Before facing him again, she pulled on her beach cover-up and wrapped it around herself until very little skin was visible.

Without a word—and with as much professional detachment as she could muster when her lips were still throbbing from his kiss and her breasts were still tingling with sensations—she stepped behind his chair and pushed it forward. They reached his room and got him from the chair to the bed without speaking. Once he was settled, she garnered enough courage to look him in the eye.

"I'm appalled because of what happened."

"You're wet because of what happened."

She gave a quick, soundless gasp, shut her eyes, and shook her head in denial of the truth. "We'll forget all about it," she said.

"I dare you to even try."

"We'll pretend it never happened."

"Impossible."

"It'll never happen again."

"Like hell."

"If it does, I'll leave."

"Liar."

"Good night."

"Sweet dreams."

She left him and went into her own room. As before, her senses were heightened. The moonlight spilling through the windows resembled molten silver. The priceless area rug felt wonderful beneath her bare feet. She sat down on the very edge of the bed, lowering herself to it carefully, as if it were a ledge overlooking a steep canyon.

Sightlessly staring into near space, she raised her hand and exploringly touched her lips. They felt swollen. She ran her tongue across her lower lip. She tasted Adam.

Her eyes slid closed, and against her stubborn will, she made a yearning sound. She hadn't believed it could ever happen, not for real, not seriously, certainly not to her. She would have felt safe betting anything dear to her that she would never get emotionally involved with a patient. That rule was on page one of the physical therapists' handbook.

Yet here she sat, her emotions jangling, her nerve ends sizzling, and there didn't seem to be a thing she could do about it.

Nothing like this had ever happened to her before. Oh, she'd had her share of fanny patters. More than one wandering hand had ventured beneath her skirt while she was giving a patient a rubdown. She'd been groped and grabbed by scores of amorous patients who fancied themselves in love with her because she was intimate with their bodies. She warded off those unsolicited passes, dismissed them as professional hazards, and forgot them almost as soon as they occurred.

This she wouldn't forget. Not soon, if ever. She wanted to deny the incident had happened. Short of that, she wanted to deny its power. But it had happened. And it had been powerful. The evidence of its potency was there. Between her thighs. On her lips. On her breasts.

She unhooked her bra and looked at her breasts. Yes, it had been real, not her imagination. There were the faint scratches his stubbled cheeks and chin had left on her skin.

The tips of her breasts were still rosy and damp and tender. She dared to touch herself.

When the telephone on the nightstand rang, she jumped as though she'd been shot. Snatching up the receiver, she shouted, "*What?* I mean, hello. I mean, Cavanaugh residence."

"Lilah? What's wrong?"

"What's wrong? I'll tell you what's wrong," she shouted crankily. "You woke me up, that's what's wrong. Do you know what time it is here?"

"No. What time is it?"

"How the hell should I know? It's late, though, isn't that enough?"

"I'm sorry," Elizabeth said contritely. "But at least I'm calling you with good news."

"The baby?" Lilah asked, suddenly switching moods.

"No, not yet. The doctor says it's still weeks away."

"How do you feel?"

"Like a blimp."

"I'll give Goodyear your name and number. They might want to use you."

"How's Adam?"

"He . . . he's, uh, fine. Fine."

"Stronger?"

Lilah swallowed, recalling the strength she'd felt pressing against her hips while sitting on his lap. "Uh, yes, definitely stronger."

"The two of you haven't murdered each other yet?"

"Not quite. We've come close."

"That's why I'm calling. We finally found a replacement."

Lilah went very still. "A replacement?"

There was a slight pause on Elizabeth's end. Then she
said, "I do have the right number, don't I? This *is* my
sister, Lilah Mason, physical therapist to Adam Cavanaugh
the hotel magnate, isn't it?"

"I'm sorry, Lizzie," Lilah said, rubbing her temple. "I
know I'm not making much sense. It's been so long since
we talked about somebody's taking over the job, I'd almost
forgotten about it."

"Forgotten about it?" Elizabeth repeated in disbelief.
"You were so adamant."

"I was . . . am." She was aggravated with herself for
not being jubilant over the replacement, but she took it out
on Elizabeth. Crossly she asked, "What's taken you so long
to find someone else?"

"We asked your supervisor at the hospital for names.
She gave us several, and we interviewed all of them, but I
couldn't see Adam with any of those we talked to. But
yesterday we interviewed a middle-aged man who comes
highly recommended. Thad and I agree that he'll do well.
He's ready, willing, and able to relocate immediately. Tomorrow, if you say so."

"I see."

"You don't sound very keen on the idea."

"Oh, I am, it's just—a middle-aged man, you say?"

"Fiftyish."

"Hmm."

"Lilah, is something wrong?"

"No, I'm just groggy. You woke me up, remember? It's going to take me awhile to digest this."

It was going to take her awhile to understand why she wasn't doing backward handsprings over the prospect of leaving Adam Cavanaugh's house as soon as tomorrow.

One, Adam and she were just becoming accustomed to each other.

Two, Adam and she were making tremendous strides toward his full recovery.

Three, Adam and she had just been necking in his wheelchair.

Lilah tried honestly to peg which of the above reasons made her most reluctant to leave him now. True, she wanted to see him through to the finish. She wanted to be the one he walked to for the first time. She wanted to experience and share in his victory over this temporary paralysis. She wanted to kiss him again.

But that wasn't going to happen.

She wouldn't let it happen. Adam's reasons for kissing her were straight out of the textbook. *Her* reasons for kissing *Adam* were too absurd to be believed. So for both those reasons she would mark down tonight as a lapse in common sense and see that nothing like it ever happened again.

That being the case, it would be stupid to sacrifice all

the progress they had made to one little indiscretion. Having to adjust to another therapist might cause Adam a severe setback. Would that be good for the patient? No. Shouldn't her decision be based on what was best for the patient? Yes.

"I don't want a replacement."

"What?" Lilah repeated her statement, more firmly the second time. "Do you realize the time and trouble Thad and I have gone to to find one?"

"I know, and I apologize."

"You could have let us know that you'd changed your mind."

"I didn't realize it until this second. Really, Lizzie, I'm sorry. Apologize to Thad too."

Elizabeth sighed with weariness. "That's okay. All those interviews made the time waiting for the baby go faster. Anyway, our hearts weren't in it. Thad and I have always thought you were the best choice. We're both glad Adam is in your capable hands."

Adam's hands were capable, too, Lilah thought. Just thinking about his stimulating caresses made her palms damp. "Well, if that's all, Lizzie, I'm going back to bed."

"You're sure you're all right? You still sound funny."

"I'm fine. Give the kids hugs for me. Kiss my good-looking brother-in-law. Bye." She hung up quickly and jerked her hand away from the phone as though it could accuse her of duplicity and manipulation.

But she couldn't as easily escape her conscience. As she

pulled back the covers of the bed and slid between them, she congratulated herself on doing something so supremely noble as staying on till the bitter end.

But secretly she knew that her motives were selfish. At least in part.

SEVEN

"*DO YOU ALWAYS SLEEP NAKED?*"

"Hmm?"

"Do you always sleep naked?"

Lilah stretched languorously between the satin sheets. She yawned broadly. Her eyes came open slowly. To a point. Then they popped wide open.

"*Adam?*"

"You remember my name. I'm flattered."

Lilah pushed the tousled hair away from her face, clutched a handful of satin to her breasts, and propped herself up on one elbow. "What are you doing in my room? How'd you get here?"

"You haven't answered my question yet."

"What question?"

"Do you always sleep—"

"Yes! Now tell me what possessed Pete to let you come in here."

"Pete doesn't know I'm here. I did it all by myself."

Amazed, Lilah peered over the edge of the bed. Adam was sitting in his wheelchair. "You got out of your bed and into the chair all by yourself?"

"Proud of me?"

"I certainly am." She flashed him a brilliant smile, but it vanished as quickly as it appeared. "That doesn't answer my question, though. What are you doing in my room?"

"Invading your privacy."

"Exactly. Would you please leave?" Something else suddenly occurred to her. "How did you know I was naked?"

"I looked under the covers." She gaped at him with disbelief, and he started laughing. "Actually, your bikini is lying on the floor, and I don't see any nightgown straps over your shoulders."

"Oh. Well, if you'd be so kind, Mr. Cavanaugh"—she coolly nodded toward the door—"I'd like to shower and dress."

"I brought you something." She had noticed the flowers, but they hadn't truly registered with her until now, when he slipped the pastel plumeria lei over her head and arranged it to his satisfaction around her neck. "Welcome to Hawaii, Lilah."

"You're several weeks late, aren't you?"

"What are you, a stickler for detail?"

Lilah looked down at the fragile, fragrant petals and

touched them reverently. They were dewy and cool against her skin. "Thank you, Adam. It's beautiful."

"You know what goes with a lei, don't you?" She glanced up quickly. Adam's eyes were twinkling. "Ah, I can see that you do."

"We'll dispense with that part of the tradition."

"That part is the reason the tradition has lasted this long. Besides, I never break with tradition."

Cupping the back of her head in his palm, he drew her forward and kissed her leisurely and expertly. "That's not the way it's done," she said when he lifted his lips off hers. "It's supposed to be a peck on both cheeks, isn't it?"

"Usually."

"I thought you never broke with tradition."

"Unless your mouth and my tongue are involved."

He kissed her again before she had the wherewithal to stave him off. Finally she mustered enough willpower to say, "Go away! I've got to get up and dress."

His eyes lowered to the sheet, which was doing a poor job of concealing the full shape of her breasts. "I think you look great the way you are. So please, don't get dressed on my account."

"Specifically on your account. It took a lot of stamina and strength for you to get out of bed alone. We need to maximize that momentum."

"I have a better idea. Let's take the day off and celebrate my progress."

"By doing what?"

He ran his thumb over her lips. "By staying in bed."

Then he raised his compelling eyes up to hers. "One bed. This bed. It's for damn sure we would maximize my momentum."

For a moment Lilah was captivated by his husky voice and enticing suggestion. Too soon, reason returned. Cantankerously she said, "Don't be ridiculous. Besides, you don't get a day off. Consequently neither do I."

He took her refusal good-naturedly and pushed his chair away from her bed. "It ain't gonna wash, Lilah."

"What?"

"Pretending that last night didn't happen. But I'm hungry for my breakfast, so for the time being I'll retreat." He spun his chair around and headed for the door. When he reached it, he glanced at her over his shoulder. "And I *did* look under the covers."

She narrowed her eyes on him. "You're bluffing, Cavanaugh."

"Oh, yeah? Love that sexy little mole just inside your bikini line," he drawled.

Before she could stammer a reply, he wheeled out. Lilah threw off the sheet and flitted across the room. She slammed the door closed and locked it, making sure both were heard. Then she stamped into the bathroom and turned on the faucets in the shower.

Adam was making a big joke out of her attitude toward last night. He thought she was being coy and wasn't taking her seriously. Last night might have appeased their libidos, but it had cost valuable ground as far as getting him to walk again. That, not romance, should be his driving force.

It was critical that she reestablish herself as his therapist, not his paramour. Desperate measures were called for.

When she entered his room an hour later, he was shooting a Nerf basketball into the goal he'd had Pete attach to the wall. "Twenty-seven straight free throws," he boasted.

Lilah walked in as stiff as a starched shirt and yanked the basketball out of his hands. "That's enough play for now. You can do that on your own time. For the next hour and a half, we're on my time." She went to the stereo system and switched it off. Whitney Houston's voice was arrested in mid-chorus.

"What's with you?" Adam asked. "Get your period?"

Lilah rounded on him. "That wouldn't be any of your business, now would it, Mr. Cavanaugh?"

"Or does your foul mood stem from sexual deprivation?"

"I'm going to ignore that."

"You can't. Not any better than you can ignore last night. Where's the lei I gave you?"

"In the refrigerator in my room."

"Why not around your neck?"

"Be reasonable. I can't wear it while we're working."

"Then when?"

"I don't know."

"Dinner tonight?"

It was time to drive the point home. "Look, Adam, it occurs to me that we've been together too much lately. A therapist should be a taskmaster, sometimes a confidante, but never a . . . a . . ."

"Lover."

"That wasn't what I was going to say."

"Oh, no?"

By an act of will she contained her temper. "We can't be such good pals, Adam."

"I've never French-kissed a pal."

"We're not sweethearts either."

"Right. We're way beyond the sweetheart stage. In fact, we're way beyond foreplay. We're ready for the real thing."

His provocative words elicited delicious little shudders inside her. Trying to ignore and deny them, she cleared her throat and said sternly, "If this goes any further, you'll lose respect for my authority. I'm asking you one last time to cease and desist making these juvenile sexual overtures. Today marks a new beginning. It's going to get tough from here."

During her speech his face had grown increasingly dark. Her temper had been close to blowing, but an eruption of his appeared imminent. By the time she finished, his fists were softly thumping the armrests of his wheelchair. "Tougher than it's been? What could be tougher than having you nag me hour after hour, forcing me to do things I can't do?"

"It's not supposed to be easy."

"Well, good!" he yelled. "Because it sure as hell isn't."

"Enough of your whining. Let's get started," she said peremptorily.

The morning therapy session was a disaster. She worked

him through a series of exercises intended to tone the muscles that were now facile. The effort he put forth was half-hearted at best. Then when she reprimanded him for his sloth, he pushed himself too hard and ended up with a cramp she had to massage out while he cursed her along with his pain. She consigned him to bed to rest, moving his wheelchair out of arm's reach, which won her even more epithets.

Of late she had loitered in his room between sessions. They watched game shows and soap operas on TV, listened to music, played board games and cards, or simply talked. Today she avoided his room until time for the afternoon session.

It went worse than the morning's. Her nerves began unraveling from the moment she went in and he said, "Don't *ever* keep my chair away from me again," until they finally became completely frazzled when he flatly refused to complete a knee exercise by saying, "I'm not going to do it anymore."

"Fine!" She withdrew her support of his leg. It landed with a thud on the mat. "As long as you feel that way about it, I think I'll take you up on that day off you referred to this morning. You reminded me that I haven't had one since I got here."

An hour later she left her bedroom suite trailing the scent of perfume in her wake. She was wearing a strapless red cotton dress that showed off her tanned shoulders and cleavage. The wrap-around skirt was narrow. The overlap formed a slit that widened to display long, shapely thighs with each step she took in strappy high heels. One side of her hair was pulled behind her ear and secured there with a large, sparkly barrette. The plumeria lei was around her neck.

When she walked into the kitchen, she dazzled both men. "Don't wait up for me, Pete. It'll probably be very late before I get back."

Adam was sitting at the table in his wheelchair, eating the cold supper Pete had prepared. She ignored him as though he weren't there. She gave the butler a gay little wave and backed out the door.

As she drove down the curving mountain road, she wondered if she had laid it on too thick.

No. Adam hadn't taken her seriously when she had told him that there could be no recurrence of last night's kiss. If she was going to succeed in getting him to walk, he must continue to think of her as his therapist and nothing more. Slave driver, yes. Cheerleader and coach, yes. But he mustn't look upon her as a playmate and love object.

Mild flirtations were fine. They served to boost his confidence and ego. Naughty bantering kept the mood light and lively. But not by any stretch of the definition did last night resemble a mild flirtation.

She ate dinner alone at an elegant Oriental restaurant, ordering courses she didn't want to drag out the meal as long as possible. She warded off the attentions of two sailors who accosted her on the street, offering her money and a night of seriously doubtful ecstasy. Purchasing two tickets at a multiscreen movie theater, she watched first one film, then moved to the next. The first was mediocre, the second nearly put her to sleep.

Having wasted sufficient time, she drove home. Quietly she let herself into the house. Standing just inside the front door, she slipped off her sandals and headed for the stairs.

Adam's wheelchair shot out of the living room and nearly collided with her. She let out a squeak of fright. "Watch that damn thing, will you?" she snapped. "You nearly ran over my foot."

"Have a good time?"

"I had a blast."

"Where'd you go?"

"To Lahaina."

"Lahaina! You drove all the way to Lahaina by yourself?"

"I've been driving by myself since the day I turned sixteen, Adam. Most places I go, I drive myself."

"Don't get smart."

"And don't get possessive. Yes, I went to Lahaina because I'd never been there. It's a nice place to visit, etcetera. I saw some charming sights, ate a wonderful dinner, and had a lot of fun. It was just the kind of diversion I needed. But it exhausted me, so I'm going to bed. Good night."

"Just a minute. Where'd you go?"

"I told you."

"I mean, where'd you have this 'lot of fun'?"

"I don't remember." She would be damned before she'd tell him she had spent the evening alone in a movie theater.

"Is your memory clouded by drink and drugs?"

"Now who's being smart? I don't remember the name of the place. What difference does it make? It had a thatched roof, I think." She searched her memory for the name of a club she had passed on the outskirts of the tourist town. "Shack something, I think."

"*The Sugar Shack!* You went into the Sugar Shack by yourself?"

"Same song, second verse."

"That's the main pickup joint on the island. You can get everything from cocaine to venereal disease in that place."

"Is this the voice of experience speaking?"

His eyes shot daggers at her through the darkness. "But you would fit right into that crowd, wouldn't you? You even dressed the part of a pickup. You blended right into the dare-anything, do-everything, what-the-hell crowd."

She tilted her head to one side and said cockily, "Let's put it this way, Daddy. I had some kicks, but I didn't meet anybody I could have a lasting relationship with."

"Did you get laid?"

Lilah went hot all over, first with embarrassment, then with rage. She was too angry to speak, so Adam used the opportunity to rub salt into the wound he'd just inflicted.

"That's what you went out for, isn't it?" He reached up and flattened his hand against her lower body. "To let some other guy put out the hot fire I stoked here last night?"

Glaring down at him, she stepped out of his reach. She removed the lei and threw it into his lap. Only then did she notice the highball glass in his hand. "You're drunk. Therefore, I'm going to ignore your cross-examination and your insults. But just for the record book, if I had gone out to get laid, as you so coarsely put it, that would be no concern of yours." She took one final dig at him from the top of the stairs. "Lord have mercy on you tomorrow if you've got a hangover."

The Lord had no mercy.

The following morning when Lilah entered Adam's room, he was propped up against the pillows of his bed wearing a green cast to his skin and a death-wish facial expression.

"No basketball this morning?" she asked in a high, piping voice. "No Whitney Houston?" Adam gave her a dangerous look from beneath his shelf of dark brows. She executed an awkward but enthusiastic pirouette and said, "I feel great! It's a positively beautiful morning. Did you have Pete's special omelet cooked in ham drippings?" Adam groaned. "It was delicious. Very cheesy. It fairly oozed when I—"

"Shut up, Lilah," he threatened between his teeth.

"Oh, what's wrong?" She pooched out her lips. "Does Adam have a tummy ache?"

"Get the hell out of here and leave me alone."

Laughing, she said, "I warned you. Don't blame me for your condition. What was it, gin? Vodka? Scotch? Brandy?" He moaned in misery and clutched his stomach. "The brandy, huh? Pretty expensive drinking binge. But then you can afford it, can't you, King Midas?"

"I'm going to murder you."

"You've got to catch me first, Cavanaugh. And you'll never do that by lying on your butt. Come on, get up, let's get started." She took his hand and tried to pull him up. He stayed glued to the pillow. "Come on, all joking aside. It's time to get started."

"I'm not moving from this spot."

Placing her hands on her hips, she gazed down at him in disgust. "Would an aspirin or two help?"

"No. Dying might."

"As far as I know, nobody has ever died of a hangover, though there have been millions of prayers to that effect I'm sure." Her voice was still brimming with good cheer. "You say another one while I get the aspirin . . . just in case God turns a deaf ear and lets you live."

She went into the bathroom and returned in under a minute carrying three aspirin tablets in one hand and a glass of water in the other. "Here you go."

"I don't want any damn aspirin."

"You'll feel much better during your workout if you take them."

"I'm not doing any exercises this morning either. I feel like crap."

"And whose fault is that?" Her patience had run out. By

this time her voice had developed a serrated cutting edge.
"Now stop behaving like a baby and take the aspirin."

She opened his hand and dropped the tablets into his
palm. He hurled them across the room. They landed on
the floor with tiny pings that might just as well have been
bombs landing and exploding. Lilah's temper snapped.
She tossed the full glass of cold water into his lap.

That got him off the pillow. He bounced up, gasping in
surprise, cursing lividly, and staring down incredulously at
the puddle of water forming in the V of his thighs. Before
he could overcome his astonishment and fury the doorbell
pealed through the house.

Pete had gone into the nearest town to do the market-
ing, so Lilah had to answer the door. Giving Adam one last
glare, she left the room and jogged down the stairs. She
pulled the wide doors open. It would have been difficult to
say which woman was more surprised to see the other.

The caller regained her voice first and asked Lilah,
"Who are you?"

"We don't want any."

"Any what?"

"Whatever it is you're peddling, lady."

The brunette drew herself up to her full height. The
skin over her face's classic bone structure smoothed out
until there wasn't a single line or wrinkle in evidence. Icily
she said, "I asked you a question, young woman."

"Now I'm asking. Who are you?"

But Lilah already knew. The pieces of luggage sur-
rounding the woman cost more than Lilah's compact car.

Her clothes didn't need visible tags to label them expensive. She had milky white skin, china blue eyes, ebony black hair, and ruby red lips.

"It's freaking Snow White," Lilah muttered.

"I beg your pardon?"

"Nothing. Come on in."

Lilah stood aside and let the woman step into the foyer. She was careful not to let her skirt brush against Lilah's bare legs, a snub that Lilah found amusing.

"Where's Pete?" she asked.

So she'd been here before. "Grocery shopping."

"Where's Adam?"

"Upstairs in his room."

"And for the final time, who are you?"

"Lilah Mason."

"Lucretia von Elsinghauer." Lilah failed to respond. Obviously she was expected to drop to her knees and genuflect. She only stared back at the woman, unimpressed and giving no ground. "What are you doing here, Miss Mason?"

Lilah lowered her eyelid in a slow, suggestive wink. "Wouldn't you just love to know?" She took a perverse pleasure in watching those facial muscles tighten up again. "Relax, Lucretia. I'm Adam's physical therapist."

The woman's chilly blue eyes moved over Lilah, taking in her bare feet, skimpy gym shorts, sleeveless T-shirt—which promoted a rock radio station—and large mismatched earrings. "I want to see Adam. Immediately," she stressed.

"Shall I lead the way?" Lilah asked sweetly.

"I know the way."

"I figured as much." She swept her arm wide to indicate the staircase.

Lucretia shouldered her Louis Vuitton handbag and started up the stairs. Just as she reached the top, Lilah called up to her from below, "Oh, maybe I should warn you. He just had an accident in his bed." She shrugged, bringing her shoulders up level with her earlobes. "Hey, it happens."

"Not good for boss," Pete pronounced philosophically, shaking his head. "She say, 'Crean up this.' Wadder all over boss. I crean. Change bed. She say, 'Now wreave.' I go. Not good for boss."

"Will you stop carrying on?" Lilah plucked a snow pea out of the salad he was making and munched on it. "You don't have to expound on Miss von Elsinghauer's personality flaws to me. She must be a descendant of Hitler's." Pete went into his knee-slapping routine that meant he found something hysterically funny. "It wasn't intended as a joke. I'm dead serious."

Lilah had known the instant she opened the door to Lucretia that her arrival boded ill for all of them. Maybe she was being unfair in her judgment, but she didn't think so. The woman had been under the roof only a few hours and had already caused discord.

After Pete had carried the wet sheets downstairs and Lilah had waited long enough for Adam and Lucretia to have a tender reunion, she knocked on his bedroom door. It was Lucretia who called out, "Come in."

For the first time since Lilah's arrival, Adam's suite resembled a sickroom. The shutters on the windows had been drawn together and closed, blocking out the scenery and all but the most tenacious slits of sunlight. Instead of the rock music that he and Lilah preferred to have blaring, chamber music was weakly wafting from the stereo speakers. The funky poster she had bought for him on her shopping expedition and placed on the wall opposite his bed had been taken down. The atmosphere was funereal.

"I'd better get a Seeing Eye dog if I'm going to find my patient in all this gloom," she quipped as she made her way toward the bed. "What the hell's wrong with you?" Having reached the side of his bed, she saw that Adam was reclining against his pillows with an ice bag sitting on his forehead.

"Adam's not feeling well." Lucretia materialized out of the shadows like a phantom.

"That's to be expected. He got stinking drunk last night. He's got a hangover, which a Bloody Mary and several aspirin would fix right up."

"I don't believe he should be given any medication until we've checked with his physicians."

"Medication! I'm talking about three measly aspirin."

"Lilah, please." Adam groaned. "Lower your voice to a shrill at least."

She leaned over him. "Would you kindly tell me what's

going down here? It's time for your session and you're playing a deathbed scene."

He covered his face with his hands and closed his fingers around his head. "Oh, God, my head is coming off."

"Too bad, Ace. It's time for your exercises."

Lucretia wedged herself between Lilah and the bed. "Surely you don't expect a man in pain to go through therapy."

"For your information, Miss von whatever, most of my patients are in pain. I help relieve their pain. At least in the long run I do. Now would you please excuse my patient and me. We've got work to do."

"Obviously you've had limited experience in your chosen field and are overzealous in carrying out your responsibilities."

Lilah gritted her teeth. "I'm a professional who has had vast experience, both with patients and with getting around their meddlesome friends and relatives and *lovers* who might mean well, but who don't know what the hell they're talking about when it comes to physical therapy."

"You boast of being a professional, but your attire and conduct might make one wonder, wouldn't it?"

"And one might find oneself getting packed off to the nearest motel if one doesn't haul one's elegant ass out of my way. Adam," Lilah snapped, "tell her to get lost until after your session."

Wearily he removed the ice bag from his forehead. He gazed back and forth between the women, but his eyes finally lighted on Lilah. "I really don't feel well, Lilah. Couldn't we skip it until after lunch?"

Blood surged through her veins in proportion to her mounting anger. She gave him a look of undiluted contempt, ignored Lucretia's smug expression, and stormed out, rattling every pane of glass in the house when she slammed the door behind her.

Now, sitting in the kitchen waiting for noontime to roll around, she still shook with rage every time she replayed the scene in her head. Pete had to repeat what he'd said several times before he roused her. "I'm sorry, what did you say?"

"Runch ready."

"Good. I'll go call them."

"That won't be necessary, Miss Mason," Lucretia said from the doorway. "I've come down for a tray. Adam prefers to eat in his room."

"Well, what Adam prefers and what Adam is going to do are two different things," Lilah said tightly as she came to her feet and faced the other woman. "He's been eating his meals downstairs for weeks. He hasn't had a tray taken to him since he learned to get in his wheelchair. He needs the exercise. He needs to be up and moving about on his own. And dammit, he's not going to lie up there and let you spoon-feed him lunch and sympathy."

"Not that I'm questioning your expertise—"

"Like hell you're not!"

"—but Adam seems completely done in. I intend to call

Dr. Arno this afternoon and ask *him* what *he* thinks Adam needs. Pete, why aren't you preparing that tray?"

"Rirah say no."

"Oh, fix the stupid tray," Lilah said angrily and marched past Lucretia out of the room.

"You're sure she understands?"

"Completely." Dr. Arno told Lilah over the telephone. "I explained to Miss von Elsinghauer how far Adam had come in the time you've been working with him. I told her that if the current pattern continues, he could be normal or near normal in a matter of weeks, but that it was vital that your program of therapy not be interrupted and that the patient's optimism be kept at a high level."

Lilah's inner tension relaxed for the first time since she had opened the door to the stunningly beautiful Lucretia. "Thanks, Bo. I was about to have a battle royal on my hands here."

"I would bet on you to win any battle you might engage in, Lilah," he said around a chuckle. "If you have any problems, please let me know. But I think we headed off a major crisis."

"Thanks again for backing me up."

As soon as she replaced the telephone receiver, she ran out of her room and into Adam's. But she was brought up short by what she saw.

Lucretia was sitting on the edge of his bed. She had changed clothes since her arrival and was now wearing linen slacks, but there still wasn't a hair out of place and she looked far from Lilah's idea of "casual."

Lucretia had Adam's hand sandwiched between hers. He was laughing up at her. It struck Lilah like a blow dart how devastatingly handsome he was when he was smiling like that. It struck her just as hard how much she had missed him. They'd spent so little time together the last two days. When they had been together, they'd been fighting.

It also hit her like a bolt of lightning that she would very much like to scratch Lucretia von Elsinghauer's eyes out, and not only because of her interference with Adam's therapy.

Lilah was jealous. Of Lucretia.

Oh, hell, she'd fallen in love.

EIGHT

WHEN LUCRETIA NOTICED LILAH STANDING in the doorway, she leaned over and kissed Adam's lips softly. "I'll see you later, darling."

Lilah's hostile gaze followed her as she left the room. When Lilah turned back toward Adam, he, too, was staring at the empty doorway Lucretia had just glided through, only his expression was wistful.

"What'd you do, send out distress signals?" Lilah asked him peevishly.

"What do you mean?"

"Didn't you send for her to come rescue you from my mean clutches?"

With no assistance from her he made it from his bed to his wheelchair. "I don't rely on other people, especially women, to bail me out of bad situations. Lucretia's arrival was a complete surprise to me."

"Does she do that often, just show up uninvited and unexpected?"

"She's an independent woman. She does what she likes." He looked up at her and added pointedly, "And she knows she has an open invitation."

"Better be careful about those open invitations, Cavanaugh. Your Lucretia might put in an appearance sometime and create an awkward scene for you."

"Like what?"

"Like finding another woman in bed with you, dimwit."

"Well," he grunted as he levered himself onto the mat table, "that wasn't even a possibility this time, was it?"

Lilah swung his legs up onto the padded table. "No, it wasn't."

"So what's your gripe?"

"Was I griping?"

"It sounded like griping."

"I don't care if you keep a harem in here to coddle and cuddle you. Just clear out all the broads when it's time for your therapy."

"One broad hardly constitutes a harem."

"One or fifty, during the sessions you're going to work like hell so we can get this over with and I can go home. You start walking, and I'm outta here. In the meantime, as long as Snow White doesn't stand in my way again, we'll get along fine."

"Snow White?"

"Never mind."

"Who am I, the prince?"

"You're Dopey."

"Well, it's easy to see who you are. You're Grumpy."

In character she said, "Your muscles and joints are stiff."

"Ouch! Stop that."

"Not a word about the pain, Cavanaugh. It's your own fault. You brought it on yourself by lying around doing nothing for two days. Now we have to regain the range of motion you'd reached before you decided to become a sluggard."

They had little to say to one another after that. Lilah didn't reduce the amount of his exercises, even though he had lost ground after two days of virtual inactivity.

"You can push harder than that, Adam." They were nearing the end of the session when she broke the silence with that sharp rebuke. Usually they joked their way through the most painful exercises, swapping insults and sexual innuendos. The silence was getting on her nerves. She felt it was necessary to reestablish a little of the camaraderie they had enjoyed before The Kiss, Lucretia's untimely arrival, and her realization that what she felt for Adam was more than professional concern. "I said push."

"I am, dammit." His teeth were already bared and his face was beaded with sweat.

"Harder."

"I can't."

"Yes, you can. Come on." He made a second effort. "Better. Good. A little harder, Adam. Higher."

"When a woman tells me to push harder and higher, I'm usually doing something much more fun."

Their eyes came together like magnets. Beneath the impact of his stare Lilah became as out of breath as he. She relaxed her resisting arms and lowered his foot to the table. "Compared to that, this isn't much fun, is it? Sorry that I can't give you a better time."

He held her stare, then gave a dismissive shrug. "It's not your fault I fell into that chasm."

Whenever he spoke of the accident, his expression became bleak and self-flagellating. Lilah was always moved to pity, knowing that he still grieved over the loss of his friends. "You've worked hard this afternoon and are due a reward."

"A massage?" he asked hopefully.

"With lotion."

"Great."

"Slip off your shorts and roll over."

He had trained himself to do that and did it very well. She complimented him as she draped him with a sheet. Feeling proud of himself, he stacked his hands beneath his cheek and watched her as she went into the bathroom. "You shocked Lucretia, you know."

"How?" She brought a damp cloth from the bathroom and began sponging his arms, legs, and back with it. After she'd blotted his skin dry, she coated her hands with unscented body lotion and began massaging it into the backs of his calves. He groaned with pleasure. His eyes closed. "Concentrate on relaxing the muscles now," she told him in an hypnotic voice. "Think about the muscles relaxing. What did Lucretia say about me?" She slipped that into the conversation casually, hoping he wouldn't pick up on her avid curiosity.

"She expected my physical therapist to have a beefy figure, blunt fingers, cropped hair. Starchy white uniform. Rubber-soled shoes. She didn't expect long legs in gym shorts, a mop of blond hair, and red toenails."

"If I'm allowed a vote, I definitely prefer the latter description over the former." She was working on the backs of his thighs and buttocks now. His sighs became deeper, more frequent, more sexual.

"Lilah, do you believe in reincarnation?"

"I'm not sure. Why?"

"Because I think I just figured out what you were in your former life."

"Oh, what?"

"I'm not sure you want to know."

She leaned down and poked his shoulder. His eyes opened. "Does my former occupation have anything to do with sins of the flesh?"

His eyes moved over her hair, which was covering his shoulder with abundant unruliness. "Strictly with sins of the flesh."

"Then I'm glad I was there."

"You're shameless," he mumbled, laughing and closing his eyes again.

Lilah liked the way his eyelashes curled against his cheeks. In fact, she liked everything about his face. She secretly admired it as her hands smoothed lotion over his back. She applied just the right amount of pressure to each muscle, alternately flexing and relaxing her fingers. To touch his skin was thrilling. His vitality could be felt in each sculpted muscle.

She got so lost in her task that she didn't hear Lucretia until the door closed behind her. Lilah hastily pulled the sheet up over Adam's naked back. "You'll have to come back later," she said testily. "We're not quite finished. I'm relaxing him."

"So I see." Despite what Lilah had just told her, Lucretia moved toward the mat table. "I have something that will relax him better than a massage. Martini, darling? Just the way you like it."

Adam propped himself up on his elbows and extended his hand to take the drink. "Thanks." He sipped. "Hmm. Perfect."

They smiled at each other, then looked at Lilah expectantly. Defensively she stood her ground. To Adam she said, "You'll need help getting back into your chair."

"Surely I can help him with that," Lucretia said smoothly.

Lilah silently consulted Adam. He was sipping his martini with a connoisseur's appreciation. She wanted to knock the glass out of his hand and wipe the silly grin off his face.

"All right." She headed for the door. "I'll see you before bedtime, Adam."

"That won't be necessary either," Lucretia told her in that modulated, Swiss-girls'-school voice Lilah had come to loathe. "I'll be sleeping in here with Adam. I'll be at his beck and call through the night. We'll alert you if you're needed. Otherwise Adam will see you tomorrow morning for his therapy session. Good evening, Miss Mason."

Lilah gave her patient a fulminating look, then slammed out the door.

"What's that?"

"What does it look like?"

"It looks like a set of parallel bars."

"Congratulations," Lilah told Adam. "You just answered the question correctly. As your prize, do you want the zirconium ring, the set of scratchproof cookwear, or the weekend getaway in the Ozarks?"

"You're a regular comedian."

"It was my sense of comic timing that earned me F's in citizenship." Lilah assembled the bars where she wanted them, then stood back and surveyed her handiwork. "There."

"What are they for?"

"Well, not for me to perform tricks on for your entertainment."

"Then, what?"

"They're for you to perform tricks on for my entertainment."

He looked shocked and frightened. "Isn't this premature? Why are you bringing them in here now?"

"Because it's time you started practicing walking on them."

"As I said, you're a regular comedian."

"I wasn't joking."

"Neither was I," he snapped. He was eyeing the contraption as though it were possessed of evil powers. "I can't do it."

"You can try."

"I'll make a damn fool of myself even trying."

She released a deep groan. "Save it, will ya, Cavanaugh? You say the same thing every time I introduce something new. The pulleys, the wheelchair, the mat table. I've heard it all before, and it's getting real old. Come on. Haul ass. Out of the bed and into the chair."

"Into the chair, fine. Even onto the mat table, fine. But don't expect me to stand on my own two feet. I can't."

"Dare you."

"What?"

She leaned down until her face was level with his. "I dare you, The Gutless Wonder, to even try."

She watched the irises of his eyes contract around the pupils. He gave her a long, measuring stare, then treated the parallel bars to another suspicious appraisal. He wet his lower lip with his tongue. "Okay. I'll try," he agreed with uncertainty. "But if I fail—"

"You'll try again."

He wheeled his chair to the end of the bars, looking dubious as to what to do next. Lilah stepped between the bars. She placed a belt around his waist and using that, hoisted him out of the chair. At the same time he pulled himself into an upright position with his arms. He supported himself between the bars while Lilah knelt down and splinted his knees with knee cages.

As she stood up, she asked, "How hard are you?"

"Pardon?"

"Your belly, Cavanaugh, your belly. Do you need an abdominal binder?"

His eyes glinted with naughty thoughts. "Touch it and see how hard it is."

"Bet you say that to all the girls," she said, responding with a naughty smile of her own.

Accepting his unspoken dare, Lilah splayed her hand over his tummy. The muscles beneath his warm, hair-dusted skin jumped reflexively. Standing close, they each felt the jolt of the contact. She pressed the pads of her fingers against him. His stomach muscles drew up taut and tight, telling her what she needed to know. The therapist in her was satisfied. But the woman in her was craving more. Lilah regretfully withdrew her hand. "You're hard all right," she said gruffly.

"Yeah. The last thing I need is something to make me harder."

They held a stare for several heartbeats. Then Lilah dragged her gaze away. "Let's begin."

"Show me what to do."

She bullied and coached and cajoled him. He shouted at her. She yelled at him. They cursed each other. But before the session was over, he had managed to shuffle his feet in a semblance of taking steps between the bars.

"Great work, Ace. You're getting the hang—"

"*Oh, my God!*"

Lucretia's shriek startled Adam and caused the muscles

in his arms to give way. He would have collapsed to the floor had Lilah not been there to break his fall. Taking all his weight upon herself, she backed him up and gradually lowered him into the wheelchair. Then she whirled around to confront Lucretia. "Get out of here! How dare you interrupt us during a session."

"You can't order me around, Miss Mason."

"I damn sure can. Mr. Cavanaugh is my responsibility. While we're in this room, his attention has to be solely on me and what we're doing."

"The fact that he's your responsibility can be remedied," Lucretia threatened in a voice that could have chilled the martinis she was so fond of mixing for Adam. "I intend to take up that very subject with his physician. Indeed, another physician is a distinct possibility. It seems to me that what you are doing for Adam at Dr. Arno's recommendation is causing more harm than good. He is obviously in pain."

Lilah whirled around to see that her patient was wearing an expression of sheer agony. "Adam?" She dropped to her knees in front of his wheelchair and began massaging his calf muscle. It was contracted into a knot as round and hard as a baseball.

Lucretia moved alongside his chair and blotted his sweating forehead with a monogrammed handkerchief. "Leave him alone now, Miss Mason. Haven't you done enough for one morning?"

"*Me?* I wasn't the one who came barging in where I

wasn't needed or wanted and caused him to break concentration."

It took several minutes, but eventually Adam's muscle returned to its normal state. His contorted facial features relaxed. But Lilah could tell that the fall had caused him as much embarrassment as pain. It had hurt his pride and bruised his ego. She could easily throttle Lucretia for undoing in a matter of seconds what it had taken her an hour to work up to. Adam's confidence was shattered. The next time she suggested using the bars, she would have to start from scratch, convincing him of his ability. Damn the woman!

"Kindly leave us," she said stiffly.

"Your time is up."

Lilah consulted the clock on the nightstand. "Can't you tell time? We've got fifteen more minutes."

"Surely you're not going to make him stand up again."

"No, we'll go through a series of exercises to relax the muscles."

"Then, I'll stay and watch."

"You'll do no such thing. This is between my patient and me. Adam, you don't want her here, do you?"

Lucretia laid her hand on his shoulder. "Don't you think it would be a good idea for me to learn how to do this?"

That infuriated Lilah even more. "We're not talking about pouring tea, Snow White. You don't learn 'to do this' in an afternoon. It takes years of study and hands-on practice to get certification."

"It can't be that difficult," Lucretia said with a soft, derisive laugh. "I should know how you do it, so that I'll be able to give Adam therapy myself once we're married."

Lilah's heart hit the floor. She gaped at Lucretia, then at Adam. "Married?" she wheezed.

"You didn't know?" Lucretia affectionately ran her fingers through Adam's hair. "Adam didn't actually propose to me until yesterday, though he was close to it the last time we were together, which was only days before his accident."

Lilah looked down at him with stark heartache and incredulity. "You asked her to marry you?"

"We're seriously talking about it."

"You actually want to marry *her*? Why?"

"I beg your pardon," Lucretia said with affront. "Adam—"

"Be quiet, Lucretia," he interrupted sharply. "I want to hear what Lilah has to say." He hadn't taken his eyes off her. They gazed up at her steadily from beneath his brows, but his expression wasn't malevolent. If anything, he seemed amused. At the very least, curious. "Why don't you think I should marry Lucretia? We've been close acquaintances for several years."

"A bit more than that, darling," Lucretia interjected. Adam shot her a warning glance to keep silent.

He turned back to Lilah. "Lucretia is sympathetic to my

present condition. However it turns out, she's reconciled to living with me."

"What do you mean by 'however it turns out'?"

"My being sexually dysfunctional."

"Is it really necessary to discuss something so personal with the hired help?" Lucretia asked with irritation.

Adam quelled her with another hard look. "I'll deal with this my own way, Lucretia. If you can't keep quiet, leave the room." She chose to stay, but her red lips drew up into a disapproving pout.

"Lucretia is willing to marry me in spite of my inability to sire children," he calmly told Lilah. "She's kind. Certainly beautiful. A cultured, congenial woman. Why wouldn't any man, but especially one in my situation, be overjoyed that she consented to marry me?"

Lilah hiked her chin up a notch and flung her hair back defiantly. "If you want to make the biggest mistake of your life, it's no skin off my nose."

Again Lucretia opened her mouth to protest, but Adam shot her a look of such dire threat that her perfect white teeth clicked shut.

"Why do you think that marriage to Lucretia would be a big mistake?"

"Remember, you asked for this," Lilah cautioned him.

"I'll remember."

"Okay," Lilah said, taking a deep breath. "She's not acting in your best interest. She's babying you, mollycoddling you, pampering and petting you."

"What's wrong with that?"

"Everything."

"You don't think husbands should be pampered?"

"Not husbands in your condition and certainly not at this stage in your treatment. Once you're back to normal, you can be waited on hand and foot, and I'll give a green light to any woman dumb enough to do that for a man. But right now, you should be driven and bullied and prodded—"

"In other words, she should treat me the same way you do."

"Exactly! What she's doing is fine if you're content to lie around and sip the martinis she brings you and eat your meals from her hand. If that's the quality of life you want, then far be it from me to argue with your decision. If you want to watch your nice hard belly turn to fat and the muscles in your legs shrivel to mush and your arms become flabby from disuse, not to mention your chin and chest, then fine. Go to the altar with her and say, 'I do.'

"But if you want to be Adam Cavanaugh, if you want to walk and jog and ski and climb mountains, which is what you told me you wanted, then you'd better set her straight or ditch her altogether."

"Adam!"

Lilah disregarded Lucretia's exclamation of outrage and drove her point home. "Before you make up your mind, though, consider this. When the ski season rolls around and all her buddies are jetting off to Saint-Moritz, where do you think that'll leave you? Huh? I'll tell you. Alone. Abandoned. Because she'll go to Saint-Moritz. And you'll urge her to go because you'll feel guilty because she's sacrificed so much for you. You'll be left cooped up in some stuffy bedroom with an even stuffier servant, who will despise and deride you for your weakness and take his sweet time in answering the tinkling little bell on your nightstand.

"While your gorgeous wife is out taking on the slopes— and probably a few ski instructors, because by now the newness of her noble gesture will have worn off and she'll be thinking that she made a bad deal—you'll be lying helpless and useless. You'll be torturing yourself, wondering who she's with and what she's doing. You'll be remembering with bitterness the days when you picked up ski bunnies and took them home to snuggle. You'll be lamenting the days when you controlled a globe-spanning corporation and left people breathless in your energetic wake.

"Eventually she'll leave you more frequently to go sailing or grouse shooting or to meet a lover, and then the day will come when it's just not chic to be married to a paraplegic anymore and she'll divorce you and probably take off with a few of your millions, which she'll feel she earned for giving you her time and trouble."

"Of all the— I won't stand here and—"

"You're free to leave anytime, Lucretia," Adam said blandly.

"What? I wouldn't think of leaving you alone with this wretched person. She's obviously unbalanced."

"I'm no such thing," Lilah shot back. "And as for being alone with him, I was here for weeks before you showed up."

Snow White's cheeks turned a deep, rosy pink. "What does she mean by that, Adam?"

"Use your imagination, Lucretia," he said.

"You actually engaged in . . . in . . ."

"Sexual dalliances. Can't you bring yourself to say it?" Lilah taunted. "He kissed me. More than once."

"Not only kissed, but enjoyed," Adam added softly. "Very much."

Lucretia was rendered speechless by the impetus behind his whispered words. So was Lilah. She locked stares with Adam and it was several moments before she could continue. "Which brings us around to the subject of sex."

"It does?" He smiled that grin, that endearing, beautiful, wonderful grin that gave his face a piratical aspect.

"That's what this is really all about, isn't it?" Lilah asked rhetorically, as though they were alone. "You're afraid that if you don't grab the first woman who is sympathetic to your condition, you might miss out on women altogether. Adam," she said earnestly, "if I thought she was sincere, I'd pin a medal of self-sacrifice on her myself. But if I were you, I'd examine why she conceded the point of not having children so quickly."

Both ignored Lucretia's gasp. Lilah plunged on. "Did you ever think that she might be relieved? Maybe she's glad she won't have a husband who'll demand that she dutifully eke out an offspring. I doubt she would want to sacrifice her figure or her time to a child. She just doesn't seem cut out to breast-feed and change diapers. And while a nanny can do one, she sure as hell can't do the other."

"Breast-feeding isn't essential," he reminded her quietly.

"To me it would be."

"Would it?"

Deep down inside, Lilah quivered. "That's not the issue. You're getting me off the track." She began again. "I don't think you'll have a single problem in your marital bed, either for recreational or procreational purposes. To any woman who truly loves you, it won't matter either way. But I know it matters to *you*. So if you're that worried about its not working, I'd rather you try it out on me before taking a chance that it won't and marrying Snow White."

A stunned silence followed. None was more stunned than Lilah. She heard her own words, but she couldn't believe that she'd spoken them. It had been an impulsive statement. Though now that she had time to review it, she realized that it was true and conveyed her deepest feelings.

She didn't mind what Lucretia thought about her speaking her heart, but she did mind what Adam thought. She couldn't bear looking into his eyes. They revealed nothing except the intensity of his reaction. But the reaction itself remained a mystery.

Turning on her bare heel, she left the room.

Several ponderously silent seconds ticked by before Lucretia daintily cleared her throat and spoke. "Can you believe that a hired person would have the gall to speak so candidly about what is absolutely none of her affair? What a trial she must have been for you, darling." She shivered with revulsion. "I'm amazed you tolerated her this long. I'll see that she's packed and out of the house by night-fall."

Adam caught her arm as she brushed past his chair. She glanced down, surprised by the strength of his grip. "Lilah won't be packing, but you will."

Her cheeks paled. "You can't be serious, Adam. Surely you didn't put stock in anything that deranged woman said? You couldn't have. You're more intelligent than that."

"I'm very intelligent. That's why I keep tabs on every acquaintance, friend, enemy." He paused before adding, "And lover." He released her arm and leaned back in his wheelchair. "Lilah didn't tell me anything I didn't already know." He smiled thoughtfully, as if momentarily distracted. "Not about you anyway."

When his attention focused back on Lucretia, his expression turned serious again. "I know about the creditors beating down your door."

"How crass of you to mention finances, Adam."

"I wouldn't if finances weren't the reason you're here." He pressed on before she could offer a lame denial. "We had some good times, Lucretia."

"Some good *sex*."

He made an offhanded gesture. "It was so easily attainable it lost its value before we ever got in bed."

"You—"

He shrugged off her scathing insult. "I was never close

to marrying you. Not by a long shot. I knew from the moment we met why you pursued me so relentlessly."

"I fell instantly in love," she cried.

"With my stock portfolio."

"That's not true. I care for you deeply. I came here to—"

"To do exactly as Lilah guessed. You wanted to smother me with your tender, loving care until I married you out of gratitude. And it would have been a bargain for both of us. I would have a wife who tolerated my incapacities. You would have a husband with the means to buy you out of hock.

"Only you miscalculated one thing," he continued. "I won't settle for being nursed the rest of my life. I've always done things for myself. I refuse to let this setback be anything but temporary. I might have to run my corporation from a wheelchair, but I'll never become a bedridden invalid content to let my brain atrophy while my *loving* wife takes advantage of me."

"You seemed to enjoy being an invalid the last couple of days," she remarked coldly.

"You caught me on an off day," he said with chagrin. "I was sulking because Lilah had spurned me. Besides, I wanted to see how far you would go. I had hoped I was wrong about you. It's a cliché, but I gave you enough rope and you hanged yourself."

"I was being put through a silly test, is that it?"

"No, actually Lilah was. She passed her test with flying colors. You flunked."

Lucretia's lip curled with contempt. "Speaking of clichés, your attraction to this foulmouthed tart is laughable and pathetic. Any man in your condition would fancy himself in love with his physical therapist."

"That's almost verbatim what she said. But I don't think either of you is right."

"And you pride yourself on your intellect," she sneered. "Don't you see that she's the only woman available to you?"

"You've been available, Lucretia," he reminded her softly. "I didn't want you, did I?"

"Bastard."

He looked taken aback. "And you accused Lilah of being foulmouthed?"

"She dresses like a whore!"

"You were the one willing to sell herself."

"I can't believe that you seriously want *her*."

"Oh, I want her," he said as a slow grin spread across his face. "And I intend to take her up on her offer."

From her bedroom window Lilah watched Pete hold open the back door of the car for a huffy Lucretia. After she had climbed in, he went around to the driver's side. Poor Pete. He would have to endure the ride to the airport in Lucretia's company. She didn't appear to be in the best of humors.

As for Lilah, her heart was soaring.

She had overcome all the obstacles standing in the way of Adam's recovery: his initial rage, his adolescent puppy love for her, his sympathetic ally. Invariably patients had a friend or spouse who countermanded the therapist's instructions. Though they were motivated by love and compassion, they were detrimental to the patient's progress.

Hopefully Adam and she had seen the last of Lucretia von Elsinghauer. It should be smooth sailing from here on.

Well, there was that one tiny personal glitch, but Lilah chose to shelve that dilemma for the time being.

She waited until the car's taillights had disappeared into the dusky twilight before she went to Adam's door and knocked. Getting his permission, she slipped inside the room. She stayed near the door, stricken by a sudden and uncharacteristic shyness.

"She's gone."

"Good riddance."

She shook her head in puzzlement. "You're not upset?"

"Vastly relieved."

"Care to explain?"

"Nope."

"Had a dilly of a fight, did ya?"

"My lips are sealed."

"Damn! I was hoping to hear all the juicy details."

"Sorry to disappoint you," Adam said, smiling hugely, "but I'll save the explanation for another time. I've had all the Lucretia I can stand for one day."

Brimming with pleasure over his words, Lilah said, "She had the house in an uproar while she was packing and making travel arrangements. I decided to postpone your session until after she left."

"I sensed that was the reason for the delay. But now that you're here, can we do the bars again?"

She thumped the side of her head with the heel of her hand. "Am I hearing right? Aren't you the patient who put up such a stink about the bars this morning?"

"I've had a change of heart."

"So I see. Well—"

"Oh, wait. Where's my poster? The one Lucretia called 'an abominable eyesore' that was desecrating my walls."

"That bitch!" Lilah exclaimed, propping her hands on her hips. "She said that about my poster? What could she find wrong with a picture of a lady and a fruit basket?"

"I don't think she objected to the subject matter. It was the juxtaposition of the lady and the banana that she found fault with."

"Some people have no taste."

"Where is it?" he asked, laughing at her exasperation.

"In my room. She told Pete to throw it away, but he passed it to me."

"Bring it back."

Looking perturbed, but actually extremely pleased, Lilah went into her room and came back with the poster. She replaced it on the nail she'd hammered into the wall herself.

When she had the frame hanging straight, Adam said, "There. Much better. Now we can get started."

They went to the bars again. His arms supported him better than during the morning session, but he relied more on his legs too. She had to coax him to quit. "Adam, you're wearing yourself out."

"Five more minutes."

"What good will you be tomorrow if you exhaust yourself tonight?"

"I'm not exhausted, I'm exhilarated."

Eventually she urged him back into his wheelchair. "Let's skip the mat table. Get back into bed. I'll give you your rubdown there. I think you could use a sponge bath too."

It was after his sponge bath and after his rubdown and when she was saying good night that he looked up at her beguilingly and asked, "What about the other?"

"The other?"

"The recreational and procreational marital bed skills I'm going to get so good at with your help." His voice dropped to a husky pitch. "When do we start working on those?"

NINE

*L*ILAH SAID NOTHING.

    For several moments he waited her out, then said, "Well?"

"Well what?"

"When do we start that therapy?" Reaching up, he curled his hand behind her neck. "I say now."

She forced a tight little laugh. "You didn't think I was serious, did you?"

His eyes narrowed and smiling, he nodded his head. "Yeah, I think you were."

"That just goes to show how wrong a person can be. I was talking off the top of my head, spouting off, letting my mouth overload my rear, as my dad used to say. It was a ploy to get rid of Snow White. I would have said anything to get rid of her. She was undoing all that we had done. She was undermining— Why are you shaking your head?"

"All those excuses are valid up to a point, Lilah, but you were emotionally involved. You were upset. Without intending to, you said exactly what was on your mind. It just popped out in the heat of the moment."

Reflexively and somewhat nervously, Lilah wet her lips. Adam ran his thumb along her lower lip behind her tongue. She angled her head back and away, but he didn't remove his hand from around her neck.

"Look, Cavanaugh, I was bluffing her, okay? Can't you take a joke?"

"I can when someone's joking. You weren't."

"How do you know?"

He sat up and leaned forward, until she could feel his breath on her face. "Because you're hot for me."

"I am not!"

"You've been running this show for weeks. I've had no choice but to let you take charge." He whisked an airy-light kiss across her lips. "This is *my* show. I'm taking over."

"I won't let—"

"Shut up, Lilah."

His hand made a yanking motion against her neck that brought her face down to his. His lips rubbed several hard, rough kisses on hers before they gentled. Sipping at her lips, he whispered, "Open your mouth."

"Adam—"

"Thanks." His tongue spiraled down into the sweet, wet heat of her mouth.

Lilah whimpered, first in protest, then in longing, finally

in gratification. Her rigid posture relaxed and she collapsed against him. The resisting muscles in her neck became pliant, so he released his hold on them and slid all ten fingers into her hair and folded them around her scalp.

Tilting his head to one side, he ate at her mouth with gentle ardor. Lilah laid her hands on his bare chest. The hair was crisp but soft. It curled around her fingers. She loved having them ensnared by it.

When they drew apart, she breathlessly spoke his name. His lips went in search of the tastiest parts of her neck. "You're a lightning rod," he said.

"Am I?" She angled her head to one side, allowing him to caress one ear with his lips and tongue.

"You attract men everywhere you go."

"Not intentionally."

"Baby, you couldn't advertise your allure any plainer if you had 'Born to Bed' tattooed on your chest."

"I don't share my favors easily."

"That's what makes you so damn sexy. You advertise it, but you don't give it away. It's enough to drive a man crazy until he gets to see you. Touch. Taste."

He groaned the last word against her lips a heartbeat before his tongue reclaimed her mouth as his possession. He reached beneath her tank top and worked the ribbed knit up and over her breasts, then pushed her far enough away from him to look at her. Her breasts were flushed and beautiful with desire. His hands cupped them. He sighed a curse.

As he tenderly massaged her, he whispered, "God, I've missed touching a woman."

He leaned forward and pressed his lips to her nipple. Lilah felt his tongue, warm and sinuous, stroking it, making it hard and ready for his damply tugging mouth.

Involuntarily her hands gripped his hair; her head fell back; she let out a soft cry. She wanted to hold his head against her forever. When he pulled away, she moaned, feeling deprived. She looked at him, glassy-eyed and bewildered. "Don't stop," she said hoarsely.

He kissed her quickly and hard. "I want to see you. Will you undress for me?"

Lilah's head cleared instantly. "Huh?"

"I'd love to undress you myself," he said ruefully, "but I want to be standing on my own two feet when I do." He kissed her again and leaving his lips against hers, whispered urgently, "Undress for me, Lilah. Make it last. Make it sexy."

She slid along the edge of the bed until her feet touched the floor and she stood up. Now was her chance. She had escaped his caressing hands and persuasive lips. This was her last chance to reestablish her professional detachment. Now was the moment to renounce the personal feelings she had for this patient. In short, it was time to turn and run.

But she stood there beside his bed as though rooted. The passionate fire in Adam's eyes, as well as her own need to love and be loved, compelled her to stay. The professional in her took a giant backward step, leaving the woman in her, which was much more vulnerable, to face this dilemma alone. There was no doubt which she would choose to do.

It had been no contest. Not really. Before she had even left his arms, she knew she would return to them. Naked and wanting.

Keeping her eyes on his, she pulled the stretchy knit tank top over her head. She held her arms high above her for several seconds before gradually lowering them and dropping the tank top on the floor. Her hair sifted back into place and settled on her bare shoulders. Adam followed each movement. His eyes glowed their approval of her breasts and their taut, coral centers.

Lilah reached behind her for the button on her shorts. Her fingers had lost their usual dexterity, but she managed to get the shorts unfastened and unzipped. She hesitated a tempting moment before inching them down over her hips, then letting them slide down her legs to the floor. She stepped out of them, leaving her in only a sheer pair of briefs. Her characteristic arrogance evaporated. Her smile was shy, half-formed, and uncertain. Terribly arousing to the man on the bed.

"Come closer," he ordered gruffly.

Lilah took hesitant baby steps to bring her even with the side of his bed and within his reach. He extended his hand and touched the faint white scar that marked her childhood appendectomy. He drew a breathtaking circle around her navel. His fingertip slowly traced the triangular perimeter of her bikini briefs. "Pretty," he said of the ice-blue lace panel and the delicate blond cloud behind it.

He slid his hand beneath the lacy elastic strip that rode her hipbone. His hand was very warm against the cool flesh it conformed to. His thumb revolved over her hipbone. Even after he withdrew his hand, he lingered to play with the lacy elastic.

"Finish."

"I . . . I can't, Adam."

"Why?"

"I'm nervous."

"Surely you've undressed in front of a man before."

She made a helpless gesture. "But it was always . . . I mean—"

"Please, Lilah."

The appeal on his face melted the last of her modesty. With only a trace of reservation she slipped her thumbs into the waistband and worked the briefs down until she could step out of them. Then she, who didn't have a single modest cell, who had always scorned those who did, who had no misgivings about the human body in any form, straightened and faced him bashfully.

Adam swore softly. "I knew you'd be beautiful, but . . ." He was too busy visually feasting on her to complete his sentence. "Lie down."

His arms, made steely and powerful because of all the demands he'd made on them lately, encircled her waist.

He drew her down and close against him. Madly he kissed her hair, her temples, her nose, her cheeks, finally her mouth.

With a low moan, he said. "Ah, that feels good."

"Nakedness?"

"No. This."

He took her hand and carried it beneath the sheet and down his body. Quite naturally and of their own accord, Lilah's fingers closed tightly around the iron warmth of his sex. He hissed another string of swear words and sought her lips with his. Their kiss was deep and hungry, their tongues carnal and selfish.

Reaching down, Adam positioned her thigh to lie over his. His palm smoothed her hip, the back of her thigh. Together they sighed.

"Can you feel that?" she wanted to know.

"I can feel the pressure. I can feel your skin. I can feel this." Slipping his hand between their bodies, he touched the feathery softness between her thighs. Her reaction was electrical. She shuddered violently.

He hesitated. "Did I hurt you?"

"No, no. You didn't hurt me at all."

She ground her forehead against his breastbone bone as his fingers pressed into her creamy softness. Clutching his shoulders so hard that her nails bit into his flesh, and squeezing her eyes closed, she surrendered to the sensations his stroking fingers evoked. She rocked her body upon his hand. Heat waves of pleasure radiated through her, each one more exquisite than the one preceding it, until she was consumed by them.

And even for moments afterward they shimmied through her, tiny shock waves of light and ecstasy.

When at last she opened her eyes and raised her head, she realized that his arms were no longer around her, but resting at his sides. He was lying against the pillows, his face expressionless and cold. His eyes were open but sightless. Worst of all, he was no longer aroused.

"Adam?" She had barely enough air to make a sound, but she knew he had heard her. He said nothing, so she repeated his name.

"You'd better leave me alone now," he said curtly. "I'm tired."

Lilah stared at him with misapprehension. Remorsefully she eased away. She paused, but when he made no move to stop her, she swung herself over the edge of the bed. Mortified and confused, she swept up her discarded clothing and fled the room.

She was glad the guest bedroom had a ceiling fan. That gave her something to stare at. She had watched it for hour after hour as the blades circled above the bed, stirring the air and drying her tears into salty tracks as they fell onto her cheeks.

She must have reviewed it at least a thousand times in her head, but she still couldn't pin down a logical explanation for Adam's behavior. His blood had been running high and hot. What had turned it so cold so fast? *What?* What had she done? What hadn't she done?

Anguished and miserable, she rolled to her side. One tear was too heavy for the fan to dry. It slid down her cheek, rolled off the tip of her nose, and splashed onto her pillow. She rebuked it . . . and all its predecessors and successors. She never cried. She never, *never* cried over a man. It made her furious that she was breaking that rule and weeping over Adam Cavanaugh. What a heartless cad he'd been to virtually kick her out of his bed.

Yet he hadn't been smug about it. It wasn't as though he had used her and disposed of her like a plastic razor. If anything, he had appeared more shattered than she. But why when she had given him what he wanted and needed, when he had proved himself capable of—

The thought crystallized and gave her pause.

Slowly she rolled to her back again. Her lips parted in surprise. Why hadn't she thought of it sooner? Clearly now, she recalled Adam's face as it had looked when she left him. Not triumphant. Quite the contrary. Failure had been stamped on his features. It wasn't that he hadn't wanted to look at her. He hadn't wanted her to look at him.

Absently she rubbed all traces of tears off her cheeks and whispered something unladylike into the darkness. "No wonder he was upset."

She knew Adam's body intimately. He had a small birthmark in the shape of Utah on the underside of his upper arm. He had stepped on a tin can at the beach when he was a kid, and the cut had left a scar on his heel. There was a dusting of soft, fuzzy body hair in the small of his back.

But just as intimately as she knew his physiology, she knew his psyche. She knew what made him tick. She knew how he thought. Given any set of circumstances, she would be able to make an educated guess what Adam's reaction would be to those circumstances.

And because she knew him so well, she now understood what had upset him.

She also realized what she would have to do about it. It would cost her some pride, but that hardly seemed of consequence when the quality of a man's life was at stake. The method she had in mind was highly unethical, surely grounds to have her license as a physical therapist revoked. Nonetheless she would do what she must. Her motivation was the strongest known to man short of survival: Love.

Lilah breezed into Adam's room the following morning, looking as chipper as Flamingo Wing lipstick and half a tube of dark-eye-circle concealer could make her look.

"Morning, Ace. How goes it?" Adam was sitting in his wheelchair, staring out the window. His mood was morose, just as she had predicted.

"Fine."

"Sleep well?"

"I slept okay."

"Pete said you didn't eat much breakfast."

"What are you, my mother?"

She laughed gustily. "Well, if I am," she said, dropping

an eyelid, "we're guilty of a grievous sin." He didn't even crack a smile. "Not funny?"

"Not funny."

"What's with you, sad sack? Need some stewed prunes?"

"You come near me with stewed prunes and I'll—"

"What? Beat me with a stick?"

"Will you just be quiet and do your job?"

"What a crosspatch," she muttered. Standing directly in front of him, she raised her arms above her head and stretched, knowing that as she did her T-shirt crept up to give Adam a view of her bare belly above her bikini swim trunks. "I slept marvelously well. Breakfast was yummy. Now I'm ready for a swim. Want to come out with me?"

"No, I'll stay here."

"And let that gorgeous tan of yours fade?" she asked in mock dismay. "I'll set up the mat table on the deck and we'll do your therapy session outside today. How 'bout it?"

"I want to work at the bars again."

"Later today."

"Why not now?"

"Because I said no."

"Because you want to slough off around my swimming pool and work on your own tan."

She thrust out one shapely hip and glared down at him. "I'm going to ignore that, Cavanaugh, even though comments like that make me madder than hell. When are you going to get it through your thick skull that I'm the therapist and you're the patient and until you can fight me down, what I say goes?"

He banged his fists on the armrests of the wheelchair and shouted, "I want out of this damn thing."

"Right," she drawled. "So we're wasting time up here arguing when we could be downstairs working on getting you out of it," she said sweetly. Stepping around him, she disengaged the brake and pushed the chair across the room and through the bedroom door.

When they reached the terrace, she poured him a glass of pineapple juice from an iced pitcher that she had prearranged with Pete to have waiting for them on the table. She kissed Adam fondly on the cheek as she handed it to him. "Maybe this will improve your mood by the time I get back."

Apparently he was too stunned by her seemingly spontaneous kiss to speak. She peeled the T-shirt over her head and dropping it negligently on the deck, strutted to the end of the diving board and executed a perfect dive that barely created a splash. After swimming several vigorous laps, she took the steps out of the shallow end and shook the water from her hair.

"That feels great! Want to sit in the shallow end?"

"I'll pass."

She shrugged indifferently. "Another time."

Adam's eyes were on her, though she pretended not to notice as she walked toward the bin where a supply of beach towels was always folded and neatly stacked. Water was beading on her skin, just as she had planned for it to. Baby oil worked miracles.

She blotted the shimmery droplets dry with the fluffy towel, then rubbed her hair with it. Keeping her back to him, she reached around and unsnapped her bra. She replaced it with the T-shirt she'd taken off only minutes earlier. The soft cotton molded to her damp skin.

When she faced Adam again, she saw that her ruse had worked. He was gripping the arms of the wheelchair so hard that his knuckles had turned white. He seemed about to come out of the wheelchair, either by a spring action device beneath the seat or by his own propulsion. His eyes were dark, smoldering with internal combustion. And he was hard. His nylon gym shorts couldn't conceal his arousal.

"I see Pete has set up your mat table." She gestured toward it. "Can you get on it by yourself?"

He wheeled his chair up to the table. Supporting himself by placing one hand on the edge of the table and the other on the arm of his wheelchair, he was able to transfer himself. Then he lifted his own legs into position.

"Soon you won't even need me." Leaning closer, Lilah added in a sultry voice, "Not for this anyway."

"I'm ready to do it."

Her eyes dropped significantly to his lap. "So I see."

"Lilah," he warned.

"Okay, okay. You're anxious to get on those bars again. But you can't blame a girl for being impressed with your other . . . accomplishments."

They went through a routine of stretching and strengthening exercises. She resisted each of his movements, and though he cursed her for her diligence, he was smiling proudly when they finished.

"Better today, right?"

"You'll be able to kick me into the pool tomorrow." She looked at him out of the corner of her eye. "Bet you'd enjoy that, wouldn't you?"

He laughed with chagrin. "More than that, I'd like to hold you under."

"Under what?"

Secretly pleased, she watched a muscle in his cheek twitch with desire and annoyance. "Under the water."

"Oh." She looked away, as though his answer had disappointed her. "Are you in a hurry to get back to your room?"

"Not especially. Why?"

"It might be nice to lie out here and sunbathe."

"Go ahead. You're off duty now."

"I meant together. Why don't you stay out here with me?"

"What for?"

"For the sun, goose. Some cultures believe that it has healing powers."

"That's superstitious bull."

"Well it certainly can't hurt," she said tartly. "But suit yourself." She spread out one of the beach towels on the deck and lay down on her stomach, but not before whipping off her T-shirt.

"What the hell!" Adam exclaimed. "Don't you have a grain of decency?"

She rolled over. "What are you hyped up about now?"

He made a waving motion down at her exposed breasts. "Pete could come out here."

"I gave Pete the day off."

"*You* gave *my* employee the day off?"

"The house is spotless, the laundry's done, I can cook. Well, enough so that we won't starve," she amended. "He wanted to go to his cousin's birthday luau. So I said yes." Before Adam could launch into a litany of protests, she slapped a tube of suntan gel into his hand. "Rub some of this on my back, will ya?"

"I can't reach you from here."

"So get down here where you can." She lay back down and returned her cheek to her stacked hands. Just as she had bargained on, he began lowering himself out of his chair and onto the deck. Weeks ago he had had to use steps in graduated heights to get from the seat of his wheelchair to the floor mats they used for some of his exercises. Now he could do it with the strength of his arms, chest, and back muscles alone. She was careful to hide her proud smile.

"Where do you want it?" he asked grouchily.

"Everywhere." Seconds later she said, "Whoa! Not so hard. And not so fast. Hmm, that's better."

Shortly, his second hand joined the first. They moved over her back with slow, smooth strokes, rubbing in the gel. Occasionally his fingertips grazed the sides of her breasts, and he would pause before resuming the massage. When she sensed that he was about to withdraw, she said, "The backs of my legs, too, please." She mumbled the request sleepily, but she'd never been so wide awake in her entire life. Her nerve endings were singing like a well-rehearsed choir.

He didn't respond to her wish right away, but hesitated for a long time. Lilah's heart nervously knocked against the deck beneath her. She clamped her eyes shut and hoped with all her might that he would do as she wanted him to, as much for his good as hers.

His better judgment gave way to his natural urges. She felt his hands on the backs of her calves. Then on her thighs. Pressing and massaging, working their way up. She had to clamp her teeth over her lower lip to keep from moaning with pleasure as his fingers gently squeezed her flesh.

Far too soon for both of them he pulled away. Lilah rolled over just far enough to allow him a peek of one breast. "Finished?" Eyes riveted to the pert, pink tip of her breast, Adam nodded. "Maybe you should have become a physical therapist," she told him huskily. "You've certainly got the touch."

Using the methods she had taught him, he maneuvered himself back to his wheelchair and hoisted himself into it. When he was situated, he looked down at her and said, "But not the callousness."

Stung, Lilah snatched up her T-shirt and held it against her chest. "I'm not callous."

"Then cruel."

"I'm not cruel either."

"Oh, no?" He wheeled his chair around, summarily turning his back on her.

"Where are you going?" she asked.

"To my room."

"I'll bring you your lunch."

"Don't bother."

"No bother. It's my duty."

"Duty be damned," he called over his shoulder. "I'd rather go hungry than be hustled by you."

His wheelchair disappeared into the shadows of the house. Lilah remained staring after him for a long time, feeling a desperate need to cry again. She was a good one for laying down plans. Too bad they always backfired in her face.

At first she couldn't identify the sound that had awakened her. Before opening her eyes, she lay motionless in her bed and swept the cobwebs of sleep from her brain. When she did open her eyes, she was surprised to see that the guest bedroom was bathed in the violet light of dusk. She had slept longer than she'd planned to.

When she had come in from the pool hours earlier, she'd been drained of energy and spirit. After a quick shower and shampoo she had barely had the strength to crawl beneath the sheet and position the pillow under her head. She'd fallen asleep instantly, being physically and emotionally exhausted after her sleepless night.

But she had intended to wake up long before now. It was way past time for Adam's session. Feeling guilty, she rolled to her back and kicked the sheet aside.

That's when she noticed the sound again. And this time recognition went through her brain like a painful splinter. "What the devil?"

Her feet hit the floor at a run. She grabbed a kimono from the end of her bed and shoved her arms through the sleeves as she dashed toward the door of her bedroom. By the time she reached Adam's room and flung open the door, she had carelessly tied the belt of the robe.

But it was still a disheveled Lilah, with hair in a tangle and eyes puffy from sleep, that he addressed from his standing position between the parallel bars. "It's about time you got here."

"Adam!" she cried, rushing forward. "What the hell do you think you're doing?"

"Watch."

She gasped softly as he bent from the waist and supporting himself with one hand, touched the floor with the other. It was a struggle, but he pulled himself erect. "How'd you learn to do that?"

"You left your book in here." He hitched his head to indicate the therapy manual lying on his nightstand. "It's to stretch the hamstrings and calf muscles."

"I know what the exercise is for," she retorted. "I also know you're not ready for it."

"Who says?"

"I do. How'd you get yourself to stand? Where are your knee cages?"

Ignoring her interrogation, he said, "Watch what else I can do. Without you I might add." He concentrated so hard that sweat popped out over his brow. The muscles of his arms and chest bulged. His thighs contracted. His efforts allowed him to take a few shuffling steps.

Lilah ducked under one of the bars and stood between them only a few inches away from him. "That's wonderful, Adam, but don't do anymore for now. You'll hurt— Adam! Did you hear what I said?"

"Yes."

"Then stop. Right there. I mean it. Don't, I said!"

He took another step. It brought him chest to chest with her. She threw her arms around his waist to lend him support. But she discovered him to be the stronger. He knotted the fingers of one hand in her hair, formed a fist, and jerked her hard against his front.

"What's your game?" he growled.

"I don't play games."

"The hell you don't. You've been playing one with me. I want to know why. Do you have a warped sense of humor? Is that how you get your jollies? Or is this give-the-gimp-a-thrill week?" He pulled her hair tight enough to bring tears to her eyes. "Why have you done everything in your female power to keep me hard?"

TEN

SMILING SEDUCTIVELY, LILAH BUMPED HER middle against his. She watched his eyes grow smoky. She came up on tiptoe and kissed his mouth. Against his lips she whispered, "I want you hard."

With a hungry sound his mouth came down on hers. He ground a savage kiss on her lips. "You knew what you were doing to me, didn't you?"

"Yes," she said defiantly.

"You tortured me intentionally."

"Not tortured, enticed."

"Why?"

"Because I want you, Adam."

He kissed her again with a release of pent-up violence, anger, and passion. His free hand raked open her kimono. He touched her breast, fanned his fingertips over her nipple, then slid his hand down the tapering shape of her body and encircled her waist with his arm. His hand splayed wide over her derriere and pulled her higher against him. When she responded with a tilt of her hips, he quickly released her.

But he was far from finished. Using his arms, he walked himself backward and dropped into his wheelchair. In a matter of moments he was in bed, lying on his back, and drawing her down on top of him.

"Give me your best, baby," he growled.

She did. They kissed endlessly, with honest, soul-bearing lust. When they finally pulled apart, he shoved the kimono off her shoulders. She shrugged out of it and stood on her knees before him, proud and unashamed. She reached for the waistband of his shorts.

In that instant she saw the first flicker of doubt appear in his eyes. He caught her hand. "Lilah, wait, I—"

She slapped his hand away and aimed her index finger at the center of his chest. "Don't you dare freeze up on me again, Adam Cavanaugh. I let you get by with it last night, but damned if I will again."

"I—"

"Shut up and listen to me." Aggravated, she ran a hand through her hair to get it off her face. "You're scared that you won't be able to see this through. But you'll never know until you try." She drew a long, unsteady breath that made her breasts quiver with emotion. "And you can lay your worries to rest that I'll taunt you if you're slow or awkward or even a total failure. I won't know the difference. I won't know if your performance is good, bad, or indifferent because . . . because you'll be my first lover."

He stared at her blankly. Seconds later, when he began to laugh, it was a nasty sound. "You lying little conniver. You've got more gall than anybody I ever met. You'll do anything, say anything, to get your patient to respond to your idea of therapy. Well, I don't want to hear your lies. And I damn sure don't want your pity."

Lilah propped her fists on her hips. "Look, Ace, there's only one way you'll ever find out if I'm lying or not."

She efficiently removed his shorts and straddled his lap. Bridging his chest with her arms, she bent low over him and swept his lips with hers. "I dare you to chance it." She kissed him in earnest, running her tongue across his teeth. "Dare you, Cavanaugh. Double dare you." Lowering her head, she nuzzled his furry chest, then touched his nipple with her parted lips. He hissed a swear word and caught double handfuls of her hair. But he didn't pull her head away, especially not when she flicked her tongue over his nipple. "Dare you."

She had barely breathed the words before he bracketed her hips between his hands and pulled her down to his rigid sex. He wasn't gentle.

Resistance.

A little gasp of pain.

He froze.

"Ah, God, Lilah. I'm sorry." His expression registered two emotions at once—regret and bewilderment. "I didn't mean to . . . I don't understand how . . . This is . . . You really are— Why didn't you tell me?"

"I did." She looked into his face. "It's the truth. You're my first. And you can believe this too. If you stop now, I'll kill you."

A smile twitched at the corner of his lips, but his touch was compassionate and tender when he reached up and stroked her cheek. "You're sure?"

"Yes." She faltered. "But I don't think I can look you in the face while we're doing it. I mean it's so . . . And I—"

"Lilah?"

"What?"

"Shut up."

He drew her down for a long kiss. His tongue made repeated forays into her mouth while his hands caressed her breasts, her back, her legs. She responded to every subtle suggestion he whispered, until, without any further pain and a great deal of sensation and joy, he was fully nestled inside her body.

He continued to coach her. A soft touch, a guiding hand, a whispered endearment. Loveplay. Sex talk. Erotic and exciting. Until it became uncertain exactly who was coaching whom.

The foundations of their worlds began to quake, then break apart. They clung to each other. He cried her name. She chanted his.

Replete, totally drained of energy, she collapsed on top of him. Her limbs were so weak she couldn't move them. Her skin was damp with perspiration. His hands continued to idly strum her back and bottom, but all she could do in reaction was smile complacently against his shoulder. It took a long time for her to regain enough strength to raise her head.

Adam was grinning.

She grinned, too, and said, "Well for starters, that wasn't bad."

". . . all I knew was that we were slipping and there wasn't anything I could do to stop it. I reached for a handhold, anything, but grabbed nothing but air. I kept saying to myself, 'Come on, Adam, *do* something. Stop this. Prevent this from happening.' I was powerless."

"And you hated that."

"Yes."

Adam sighed as he mindlessly sifted his fingers through Lilah's hair, which was spread out over his chest like a blanket. "I remember hearing Pierre scream. Or maybe it was Alex. Or maybe it was my own screams, because I was told later that they died instantly."

"Were you in pain?" Talking about his accident was therapeutic. As difficult as it was for him, Lilah had encouraged him to verbally air his feelings about it.

"I don't think so. I don't remember having any pain then. Maybe I was in shock."

"Probably."

"I drifted in and out of consciousness. I couldn't see either of my friends, but I remember calling their names and getting no answer. I think I cried."

She held him tight for several moments. He cleared his throat before speaking again. "The next memory I have is of the helicopter carrying me to the hospital. The racket was terrible. I sensed the urgency in the people around me. When I fully regained consciousness, I was told that I'd had surgery to repair the broken bones in my back."

"I'm very sorry," she told him as she laid a loving kiss on his chest. "It must have been a terrifying experience."

"I don't remember being scared so much as I was angry. It was happening to *me*, and I couldn't quite believe that. I had so much I still wanted to do with my life." He shook his head in befuddlement. "I know that was a crazy thing to be thinking at the time, but that's what was going through my mind."

"You felt, 'How unfair,' right?"

He laid his hand heavily on her head. "Yeah. That's it in a nutshell. Tragedies were supposed to happen to other people. Not to Adam Cavanaugh. I heard hard luck stories on the news, but I went on with my life untouched and unscathed. Doesn't make me sound like a very nice fellow, does it?"

She stacked her fists on his breastbone and propped her chin on top of them. Gazing up at him, she said, "It makes you normal. That's what everybody in your predicament feels like. The 'why me?' syndrome. And it's justified. *Why* you?"

His expression was reflective. "I don't know. Was God favoring me or punishing me? I thought about that a lot when I first regained consciousness. Why was I the one who survived?"

"Don't feel guilty for surviving. Aha, you already have," she said, reading his rueful expression correctly. "Sometimes the survivors have the hardest time of it."

"I thought about that too. Especially before I was brought here. I hated lying there in the hospital in Rome, helpless, in pain, unable to move, afraid."

"What were you most afraid of?"

He thought for a moment before answering. "I was afraid of never being Adam Cavanaugh again. I felt like I'd been robbed not only of the ability to move, but of my whole identity."

"That's symptomatic of your condition too." She kissed him lightly on the lips. "What is it? You have an odd smile on your face."

"I know this sounds stupid, but I was embarrassed too. The first time they put me on that . . ." He made a descriptive motion with his hands.

"The tilt table."

"Yeah. I threw up all over myself. Imagine, Adam Cavanaugh, CEO of the worldwide Hotel Cavanaugh chain, disgracing himself like that."

She inched upward and kissed him again, more soundly this time. "You were the only one there who was unsympathetic with your condition."

"I know. I gave everyone a hard time."

"No foolin'."

He laughed with chagrin, but became serious again. "One of my character flaws is that I have no tolerance for personal failings."

"You have no tolerance for things beyond your control."

He looked down his nose at her. "I think you fall into that category. You're way beyond my control."

She giggled. "That's why you don't like me."

"I like you." He spoke with a soft earnestness that immediately captured her attention.

"You do? Since when?"

"Since . . . I don't know."

"Bet I know. You started liking me when I stripped off your shorts and jumped on your bones."

"No. I mean, yes, I liked that. A lot," he said with a lecherous twinkle in his eyes. "But it just occurred to me a second ago that I like *you*, the person, too."

"Why?"

"I guess because you've patiently listened while I've talked about the accident."

Her fingernail rimmed his lips. "I'm glad you shared it with me. You've needed to talk it out with someone. They told me that you refused counseling in the hospital."

He shrugged. "I felt like a dope."

"You're too tough to ask for help, right?" She asked it teasingly enough to make him smile.

"Thanks for listening and for not making judgments, Lilah."

"You're welcome."

He reached up and curled a wisp of her hair around his

finger. "We've gotten into some heavy subject matter here, but I find it hard to wax philosophic when a sexy broad is sprawled across my belly."

"Do you now?"

"Hmm." He regarded her with open curiosity and interest. "*But*, now that I've revealed all my secrets to you, let's turn the tables. Tell me why and how."

Assuming a casual air, she lightly plucked at his earlobe. As earlobes went, it was nice but didn't warrant the single-minded attention she gave to it. "Why and how what?"

"Why you're still a virgin—"

"How soon you forget."

He frowned at her. "Why you're still a virgin and how that's even possible."

"Technically, it's possible because I've never had a consummated love affair."

"That answers the second half of the question. What about the first half? To refresh your memory, it's the part about why."

"I never wanted to before."

"Lilah." He sounded like a parent scolding a child who was obviously stretching the truth. "I want the truth."

"That is the truth. Knowing me as well as you do, do you think I'd preserve my virginity for any other reason?"

He still seemed puzzled. "It just doesn't jive with your personality. You'll do or say anything without a single qualm. I find it hard to believe you have such a liberated and relaxed attitude toward sex but have never participated."

"I go to football games and cheer on the players, but I've never played myself."

"That's hardly a correlation."

She sighed with exasperation. "What do you suggest, that I brand a big red V on my forehead?"

He linked his hands at the small of her back and held her tightly. Nuzzling her neck, he said, "It's too late now."

"That's right. So why are you making such a big deal out of it?"

"I was surprised. No, *shocked* is a better word. And you still haven't given me a straight answer."

"I never wanted to make love before. It's as simple as that."

He was already shaking his head. "No, it goes deeper." He tried to delve into her eyes and find the truth, but she wouldn't hold eye contact long enough. "Does this have anything to do with that conversation we had about your feelings of inadequacy?"

"Of course not!"

"Bingo."

She glared at him. "Okay, maybe it does, what of it?"

"You're a beautiful, funny, sensual, sexy woman, that's what of it. Why have you deprived yourself of the most fulfilling experience the human being can enjoy?"

"Because if there was a way to mess up the most fulfilling experience the human being can enjoy, I would have found it."

Adam softened his tone. "Care to expound?"

"No, but I will since I get the impression you're going to persist until I do."

"Right."

She drew a deep breath of resignation and expulsed it slowly. "I figured that I would be as clumsy and awkward about sex as I was about everything else. I don't mean in bed exactly. I mean all the trappings that go with it. I was afraid I'd get pregnant despite precautions. I'd be the one and a half percent the pills didn't work on. I was afraid that I'd fall in love with the guy but he wouldn't fall in love with me, or the reverse." Her wide blue eyes appealed to him to understand. "I know it sounds ridiculous now, but I'd flubbed everything else I had ever tried."

"Except basketball and tennis. Elizabeth told me."

"Well, I was okay skillwise, but I got kicked off the high school basketball team."

"Dare I ask why?"

"For sewing a row of sequins on the hem of my trunks. Well, those uniforms were *ugly*, Adam," she stressed when he burst out laughing. "And men would get mad as hell when I beat them at tennis, so I quit playing. See? It followed that I'd fail at sex too."

A trace of vulnerability had crept into her voice, though she was unaware of it. "I didn't want another failure on my record. By the time I was old enough to say yea or nay to any guy who happened to ask, Elizabeth was married to John Burke. She was the perfect little homemaker. Her husband adored her. She gave birth to absolutely gorgeous, precious, precocious babies. If I had entered into a relationship with a man, it would end in some kind of dreadful tangle."

"But you dated."

"Yes, lots of men. But I always halted them before the final countdown."

"Poor suckers."

"Hey, the dates didn't come with a guarantee for goodies. It wasn't as though I made promises and then welshed. I didn't love any of them, so I didn't care if they read the signals wrong then ranted and raved, called me names, went away in a huff, and never asked me out again."

"But Lilah, the way you act, the way you talk, you can't blame a man for feeling manipulated if you don't come through."

"I guess not," she admitted. "But there was too much at stake. Everything I was, everything that makes me Lilah was at risk, and I just never thought it was a risk worth taking." Her gaze grew lambent. "At least, not until this afternoon. Now I know what I've been missing."

"Don't look at me like that, you little hustler. You should have gone into advertising. You sure as hell know how to package the product and launch a convincing campaign. You've turned a self-defense mechanism into an art form." His eyes moved over her, taking in the tousled hair, her lips, which were rouged by his kisses, the I'm-game-for-anything glint in her eyes. "God, you're sexy."

"You thought I was an easy lay."

"Certainly not easy," he said, chuckling, "but definitely worth the trouble." He pressed his palms over her derriere. "With your lusty nature you were loaded and primed. No wonder you were so quick to fire yesterday."

Lilah actually blushed. "What you were doing to me, I couldn't help it." His mouth spread into a wide grin. "Proud of yourself, are you, Cavanaugh? Well, don't get smug. As you've so ungallantly put it, I was primed. Any man could have pulled the trigger."

"But you didn't let any other man," he reminded her softly. "You let me. Why?"

Smoothing his eyebrow with the pad of her thumb, she thoughtfully considered her answer. "Maybe I knew you'd be grateful for a guinea pig and wouldn't mind my amateur performance. In fact, I knew you'd feel more self-confident with an amateur."

"You're no amateur. You're a natural. I feel sorry for all those poor slobs who tried to bed you and failed. But I'm glad they did."

He cupped the back of her head and forced her face down to his. With their lips pressed together hard, his tongue boldly entered her mouth. He separated her thighs with caressing hands. His touch was delicate and deliberate and deadly to her senses.

"Adam," she said on a ragged sigh, "can we do it again? Once more with feeling."

"Yes, yes," he moaned. "I can do it again. Now I know I can do anything."

* * *

His self-confidence hadn't flagged when he woke up the following morning. He tossed back the covers and for a second, intended to swing his legs over the edge of the bed and do some calisthenics as he had done every morning of his adult life until his accident.

With the return of awareness there usually came a depression too. This morning, however, he smiled and willed away that depression.

He was invincible. He could do anything. He had successfully made love to a woman. The return of sexual facility was only the beginning. He would soon be able to walk. Then to run. And it was all because of the woman lying beside him.

With a fond smile he turned his head and was disappointed to see that Lilah was no longer there. All night they had remained coiled together on the narrow hospital bed. The pillow bore the imprint of her head, the sheets the scent of her body, but sometime in the wee hours of the morning, after he'd finally fallen asleep from sheer exhaustion, she had evidently sneaked back to her own room.

Adam laughed to himself. If she had done that for Pete's benefit, she was wasting her time. Weeks ago Pete had dispensed some unsolicited advice, telling his boss that he should "Keep Rirah in bed. Make rove all day. Then she not talk so much, not be so wired."

Adam laughed again, this time out loud, thinking about all the times last night when Lilah had opened her mouth to speak only to have it stoppered by one of his kisses.

Frequently he had kissed her into silence. Or near silence. She made that little catchy sound in her throat that never failed to arouse him. Just thinking about it made the blood in his loins grow thick and warm.

As for being wild, she was a tigress of a lover. When stroked, she purred. When excited, she snarled. God forbid that she ever be tamed.

Lilah a virgin, he thought, chuckling and shaking his head in patent disbelief.

He worked his shorts up his legs. Wearing nothing more, he hoisted himself into his chair. He didn't even have to think about the movements anymore. They had gone from seemingly impossible to second nature under Lilah's incessant instruction. Often he had wanted to banish her from the planet when she nagged him to do one more despised exercise. Now he was grateful for her dictatorship. Look at all she'd done for him.

When he entered the hall, he glanced at her door and saw that it was closed. He aimed his chair in the opposite direction, toward the elevator, and rode it down to the first floor. Pete wasn't in the kitchen nor in his apartment.

"Crafty little booger," Adam muttered with a smile. Pete was giving them plenty of time alone together. Adam wouldn't be surprised if Lilah had arranged that too.

He made coffee and put it on a tray with two cups and two Danish. Breakfast in bed. Once they'd disposed of the coffee and Danish, he'd have dessert. Lilah. Naked and wanton and willing.

He was roused from his fantasy by his own groan of

desire. His thoughts had turned deliciously dirty. It felt so damn good to plan a seduction that he knew he could consummate.

After a hasty trip outside to the terrace to pick a giant red hibiscus bloom that would look great in Lilah's hair, among other places on her body, he placed the tray on his lap and returned upstairs. He didn't knock on her bedroom door, but backed his chair against it and turned the knob.

When he wheeled around, wearing the idiotic grin of the drastically smitten, he was met with a disappointment equivalent to a deathblow.

No Lilah. No evidence of Lilah. No evidence that Lilah had ever existed.

The room was as spotlessly sterile as the day she had moved in. The bedspread had nary a wrinkle. There wasn't an assortment of sandals scattered helter-skelter across the carpet; no lacy lingerie dripping out of open drawers. The air bore the odor of desertion, not the scent of perfume. The lacquered dresser top wasn't filmed with dusting powder. There was no array of cosmetics and loose pieces of jewelry littering its smooth, polished surface. Adam knew without looking that the closet would be empty too. The room was absent life, absent Lilah.

His roar of outrage had origins in his gut. It rumbled inside his chest, gaining impetus, and echoed through the empty house like a night cry in the jungle. It was punctuated by the crash of the carafe of hot coffee striking the far wall.

ELEVEN

"I CAN'T BELIEVE YOU JUST LEFT."

"Well, I did."

"Without saying anything? Without letting anyone know where you were going?"

Lilah wore a strained expression. She had been undergoing Elizabeth's cross-examination for the last half hour and she was weary of it. "I've told you I was in San Francisco."

"How were we supposed to know that?"

"You weren't!" Lilah shouted. "That was the point. I wanted to get away by myself for a while. I'm a big girl. I didn't know I needed anyone's permission to take a vacation."

Thad held up his hand to silence his wife's next contribution to the argument. "We understand and appreciate your need for a vacation, Lilah. But you must admit that your timing was a bit off."

"Impulsiveness is one of my traits."

Why didn't they just go home and leave her alone, she thought. She still didn't feel like seeing anyone. She certainly wasn't up to justifying her most recent escapade. She couldn't reconcile her reason for fleeing Adam's house to herself, much less explain it to anyone else.

"Impulsiveness is running neck and neck with irresponsibility this time," Elizabeth said chastisingly. "You deserted Adam when he needed you most. Without a word. Without the courtesy of a formal resignation or a simple good-bye, you walked out."

"Adam will survive. He told me so himself. Before I left he said he could do anything. I believe him."

"But your job wasn't finished. He still needed you."

Lilah shook her head adamantly. "Not me. A therapist. Any therapist would do. He'd had an attitude turnaround. He was doing amazingly well. Before I left Oahu, I stopped by to see Dr. Arno. He assured me that he could find an excellent replacement immediately."

"From what I hear, Dr. Arno came through," Thad told them. "By all reports Adam is doing exceptionally well. He's even resumed control of his corporation."

"There, you see," Lilah said, "all's well."

"That still doesn't excuse you from being derelict in your duties."

"So don't pay me. I got a great vacation out of it. I had a helluva good time."

"Don't be flippant with me, Lilah."

"Then don't be so bloody self-righteous," she snapped. "I got tired of being stuck up there on that tropical mountain. I needed a change of scenery."

"So why San Francisco?"

"I'd never been there. I wanted to see it."

Actually it was the first city she'd come to after her midnight flight from Honolulu. It was as good a place as any to lose herself and nurse her misery. She'd seen very little of the city, spending most of her time in a hotel room. But she didn't want them to know that.

"What were you doing there all that time?" Elizabeth asked her.

"Having a wonderful time."

"Alone?"

"I didn't say I was alone."

"You said you went there to be alone."

"So I changed my mind," Lilah said testily.

"Were you with a man?"

These days, Lilah's control over her temper was tenuous at best. Her dark mood hadn't improved when, immediately upon her arrival home, Elizabeth and Thad had showed up on her doorstep. "Have you had spies on the lookout for me?" she had asked when she ungraciously invited them in. From there the conversation had deteriorated. Now she confronted her sister with full-fledged animosity. "What business is it of yours if I spent the time in San Francisco with one man or with a dozen men?"

"Oh, Lilah." Elizabeth burst into tears. Thad rushed to assist her into the nearest chair.

"Don't get upset, Elizabeth. It isn't good for you or the baby."

"How can I keep from getting upset? My totally irresponsible sister has been on a two-week-long sexual spree in San Francisco. What's the matter with her?"

"You've always said she was flighty and weird."

"She should have grown out of that stage by now. She's worse than ever. Why?"

"PMS?" Thad guessed.

"I have an excellent idea," Lilah interrupted with false sweetness. "If the two of you are going to discuss me as if I were an invisible third party, I wish you'd go home to do it. I'm tired. I want to unpack. I need to telephone the hospital and tell them I'm ready to go back to work. To be blunt, I want you to leave."

Elizabeth looked wounded, but she stood up. "Gladly. But I need to use your bathroom first."

"Help yourself." Lilah indicated the way with a wide sweep of her arm.

After Elizabeth had left the room, Lilah turned and discovered that Thad was watching her closely. She sat down opposite him, but found his stare disconcerting.

He was first to break the uncomfortably long silence. "You've always been flighty and weird, but I still like you."

His statement echoed words that she'd heard recently. The memory was bittersweet. She felt tears smarting in her eyes, but she forced herself to laugh. "Thanks. I think."

He leaned back in his chair and linked his hands behind his head. "You know, it's strange."

"What is?"

"That you're so touchy tonight, coming off a vacation and all."

"Travel is tiring."

"No, the strangeness is the coincidence of it. I've spoken with Adam numerous times the last couple of weeks, and each time he's been real touchy too. He doesn't sound happy, but he tells me he's happy. In fact, it seemed important to him to convince me of his happiness. Kinda like you've been with Elizabeth and me tonight."

"I'm very happy."

"Uh-huh," Thad said with a guileless smile. "And whatever has made you so happy must be the same thing that made Adam so happy. In any event you two are just about the happiest people I ever saw. What I'm wondering is why you're going to such great lengths to make sure everybody knows it."

Thad looked at her compassionately. Lilah really felt like crying then. But she didn't have a chance. Elizabeth stepped between them and calmly announced, "My water just broke."

They both jumped as though she had opened fire on them with an Uzi. Thad bounded to his feet and gripped her shoulders. "Are you sure? Are you all right? What should we do?"

"We should go to the hospital and have a baby," she told him, laughing. "Lilah, Mrs. Alder is with Megan and Matt. Please call and ask if she would mind spending the night."

"Sure, sure. Anything else?"

"Yes, pry Thad's hands off my shoulders. He's cutting off my circulation."

With her typical aplomb Elizabeth gave birth to a baby girl shortly before dawn the following morning.

"You're so tiny," Lilah whispered with hushed reverence. "So soft." She rubbed her cheek against her niece's fuzzy head. Holding the baby in the crook of her arm, Lilah marveled over the miracle of such a small life. "Don't worry. When your mother starts dressing you in pinafores with bears and ducks and stuff appliquéd on them, Aunt Lilah will come to the rescue. I'll buy you something really funky to wear."

The baby's bud of a mouth blew a bubble. Lilah took that as approval of her idea. She was laughing when the hospital room door swished open. Her smile instantly vanished when she saw him. He was supporting himself on a crutch with one hand and holding a bouquet of fresh flowers in the other.

Adam's face registered the same degree of astonishment when he saw Lilah, sitting on the edge of the hospital bed, holding the infant against her breasts. But only momentarily. Then his features turned stony and hostile. "I was expecting Elizabeth."

"Well aren't you lucky? You got me instead."

"What are you doing here?"

"I could ask you the same question."

"I asked first."

She surrendered with a shrug that said the standoff wasn't worth the bother. She hoped he didn't notice her shortness of breath. "I'm here because of one of those hospital snafus that invariably happens at checkout time. The baby had already been delivered to the proud parents when the bookkeeping glitch was discovered. So Lizzie and Thad went to get it straightened out and asked me to stay with the baby."

"They must not love her very much."

"What a wretched thing to say!"

He didn't apologize. Instead he hobbled farther into the room and laid the bouquet on the bedside table. "What's her name?"

"Milly."

"Milly, huh? Cute. How much did she weigh?"

"Eight pounds five ounces. Where's your wheelchair?"

"Over eight pounds? Wow. I don't need that damn chair anymore."

"What are you doing on a crutch?"

"I'm walking now."

"On one crutch? Without braces? Has that therapist of yours got grits for brains?"

"He seemed to think I was ready."

"Well, I don't."

"But you aren't my therapist any longer, are you?" His

voice was silky, but his eyes were razorsharp. "How'd they decide on Milly?"

"Huh? Oh, they let Matt name her."

"Matt?"

"He was upset because she wasn't a he. He would have preferred a brother. To pacify him they let him name her. He came up with Milly because it went so well with Matt and Megan. All *M*'s, you see. It's a little too cute to suit my taste, but then they're not . . . Look, I might not be your therapist any longer, but I know good medical advice from bad, and I don't think you're ready for crutch*es*, much less one crutch."

"How would you know what I'm ready for? You haven't even seen me in two weeks and three days."

Seven hours and fifty-two minutes, Lilah could have added, but didn't. Instead she said, "You haven't had time to strengthen those muscles enough to support you."

"I've been working night and day."

"Another mistake on the part of the therapist. I knew Bo Arno was a quack," she fumed. "If you rush those muscles you could get a sprain or tear them completely. You shouldn't force them to do what they're not ready for."

"You seemed to know instinctively what I was ready for." His dark eyes penetrated hers. "Didn't you?"

Milly flailed her arms, socking her aunt on the chin. Lilah mentally thanked her. She was grateful for the diversion, a reason to look away. While she was at it, she seized the opportunity to change the subject too.

"How did you do on the long flight?"

"I made it okay," he said. "The flight crew took good care of me."

Her head came around with a jerk. His cocky smile made her want to grind her teeth. "I'll bet."

"Great bunch of ladies. They were very good about helping me in and out of my seat. Working cramps out of my legs. Stimulating my blood flow."

"How nice," she said tightly.

"Yes, it was."

"You could have waited, you know. Elizabeth and Thad would have understood. You didn't have to rush across the ocean just to see Milly."

"I'm her godfather. I couldn't wait to see her."

"Even if it causes a relapse and puts you back in a wheelchair?"

"I'll never go back into a wheelchair. That leaves you at the mercy of some very unscrupulous, untrustworthy people."

"Meaning me, I suppose?"

"If the shoe fits."

"Go to hell."

Milly protested the shouting match by setting up a wail. Lilah began to rock her in the cradle of her arms. The baby continued to cry. She glared up at Adam. "Now look what you've done."

He moved to the edge of the bed and eased down, propping his crutch against the mattress. "Don't you have any maternal instincts?"

"Yes, of course I do. Every woman does."

"Then make her stop crying."

"What do you suggest?"

"Maybe she's wet."

"Thad already took the diapers to the car."

"Maybe she's hungry."

"She's out of luck there too. I'm not properly equipped."

"You're equipped."

Their eyes met. For a moment a soft, melting look replaced the antagonistic ones they'd been exchanging. They recalled the times when his mouth had tugged fervently at her breasts.

Lilah forced herself to look away, fearing that if she didn't, she would collapse against him and beg him to hold her and never let go.

"She's quieting down," she needlessly observed.

"Yeah."

When Milly's fussing subsided, Lilah studied his face closely. "You look tired."

"I've seen you look better too."

"Thanks." She smiled crookedly. "I can't even take umbrage because I know you're right. The last few days have been hectic. I've been running errands for Lizzie and trying to keep Thad anchored to earth and relieving Mrs. Alder, their sitter. Megan and Matt have been as wild as Indians, feeling threatened by the new baby, I'm sure. They're making certain they retain everybody's attention by behaving like hellions."

"You're into all that psychology, aren't you?"

Something in the way he asked it immediately set her teeth on edge. "Sometimes," she answered evenly.

"But especially with your patients. You figure out what they need and you give it to them, whether it be humor or scolding or . . . anything."

"If you have something on your mind, Cavanaugh, why don't you just come right out and say it?"

"All right. Why did you run out on me?"

"I had accomplished what I set out to."

"Seduce me?"

Her eyes got stormy. "Get you to walk."

"I wasn't walking yet."

"But you were close. The morning I left you said yourself that you could do anything. You didn't need me anymore."

"Wasn't that for the doctors to decide? Or me? Or are you just naturally smarter than everybody else?"

"I wasn't going to stick around just to get canned."

"At a thousand bucks a day!?" he cried incredulously. "You must have had a good reason to give that up."

"I was tired of so much bloody good weather."

"Why did you go to bed with me, Lilah?" he asked abruptly. "Going-away present? Were you a merit badge I earned? Or was I one you had earned?"

She reacted as though he'd slapped her. "How dare you say something like that."

"Then why? Tell me."

"I knew you needed proof that you were a whole man."

He laughed, but it was a humorless noise. "Isn't that

going above and beyond the call? All young male patients are worried about that. And we both know you haven't provided them with proof. What made me different? Why did you sleep with me?"

"Because I wanted to," she shouted. Baby Milly flinched at the sudden noise.

"Why?"

"Curiosity," she said breezily. "It was long overdue. I wanted to see what all the fuss was about."

"Liar." Her jaw dropped open. "You were responding to the chemistry that has arced between us since the first time we met," Adam said, moving his face closer to hers. "Ever since you said, 'How do I do what?' I've wanted to take you to bed and find out. You were attracted to me, too, even though both of us refused to admit it.

"But it finally happened. We surrendered to it, and it was great, but it scared hell out of you. Because you've successfully bluffed your way through every other relationship in your life, you couldn't handle the real thing. When you discovered what all your sexy back talk was really about, you tucked tail and ran."

"You're full of crap, Cavanaugh."

"You're a coward. You ran out before something could go wrong."

"And why not? I wasn't about to stick around, nursing you along until you could go running back to Snow White von Elsinghouse—"

"Hauer. Von Elsing*hauer.*"

"Whatever. I wasn't going to watch you go running back

to her on winged feet!" To her acute mortification, Lilah realized she was crying. She angrily rubbed the tears off her face. "Damn you, you Irish idiot! You know why I went to bed with you. I fell in love with you. And yes, I would have done anything, anything, to give you back the use of your legs and the lifestyle you had before.

"More than I wanted my next breath, I wanted to watch you take your first steps to me. But I didn't want to watch you walk *away*. I was not going to stay with you and be disposed of when you didn't need me any longer. I wasn't going to let you go on making love to me, mistaking gratitude for grand passion and honing skills to be used on other women. And finally, I don't think you're ready for crutches yet. Don't you know the damage you could be—"

"Lilah."

"—doing to yourself? You fool. And that—"

"Lilah."

"—therapist who replaced me must be a fool too. Because any expert would agree that you're rushing it."

"Lilah."

"Another thing," she said, taking a swipe at her flooding eyes, "I knew something would go wrong if I ever slept with a man. Sure enough something has. My period is already a week late. I could kill you, Cavanaugh!"

He squeezed her jaw between his fingers. "Dammit, I've only found one means of effectively shutting you up."

He pressed his mouth against hers. That's all it took. A heartbeat later they were arcing over baby Milly to kiss each other ravenously. Finally tearing his mouth away, Adam snarled, "I should strangle you for putting me through such hell. Don't you ever leave me like that again. Never."

"Did you miss me?"

"Hell, no. I missed the clutter and the noise and the absolute chaos that surrounds you."

"You missed having someone around to fight with."

"Hmm. I like fighting with you."

"Really? Why?"

"Because when you get mad, your breasts jiggle." He reached around the baby and beneath her sweater to press the raised center of her breast with his palm. "It's enough to give a dead man a—"

"Are we interrupting?"

Lilah and Adam turned toward the door. The Randolphs were standing there. Elizabeth was staring at them wide-eyed and flabbergasted. Thad was trying to contain a boisterous laugh. Adam withdrew his hand from beneath Lilah's sweater but he was in no hurry.

The four of them didn't quite know how to cover the awkward moment. Finally Lilah said, "Well, don't just stand there gawking. Come get the kid so Adam and I can go to my apartment and diddle."

"What am I going to do with your fresh mouth?"

Lilah's grin was unmitigatedly wicked. "I have a wonderful idea."

He looked at her warily. "I don't want to hear it."

"Yes, you do. You're dying to hear it." She whispered her idea in his ear and the rim of it turned red.

"You're right," he said huskily, "that is a wonderful idea. We'll jump right to it as soon as we get a few things settled. Like what I'm going to do about your fresh mouth when we're not lying naked in bed and there are other people around. Important, stately, dignified, moneyed people who patronize my hotels."

"Am I going to be around that much?"

"If you're Mrs. Adam Cavanaugh, you're going to stick to me like glue."

"Am I going to be Mrs. Adam Cavanaugh?"

"Damn right. A period that's a week late is grounds for marriage if I ever heard one."

"Is that the only reason you're marrying me?"

"You don't think I'd marry you if I didn't have to, do you?" Sinuously, she rubbed her body against his. He groaned. "On second thought, maybe I would." She smoothed her hand down his front. He grunted with pleasure when she found him smooth and taut with arousal. "Okay, okay, I'd marry you anyway."

She brushed her lips back and forth across his. "And I promise to always be nice."

"Not too nice, I hope. Just warn me before you do or say something really outrageous so I can hide. And never, *never* be nice in bed." He rolled her to her back and braced himself above her.

"Nice trick, Ace," she quipped, smiling up at him. "Who taught you that?"

"A real pain in the butt therapist I once had."

"As I recall, you were the one with the pain in the butt. Remember those decubitus ulcers?"

"The bedsores?"

"All gone now." She ran her hands over his buttocks. They kissed. When he finally raised his head, his eyes were troubled. "What?" she asked quickly. "Are you in pain?"

He shook his head. "No, no, it's not that." He gazed beyond her head for a moment before bringing his eyes back to hers. "My prognosis is still uncertain, Lilah. I saw Arno the other day. He put me through a battery of tests. He's still convinced that one day I'll be as good as new, but there's an outside chance that I might always walk with a cane, with a pronounced limp.

"I think if I had had to, I would have thrown down that crutch and chased you through the hospital corridors until I caught you." He paused. "But I might never be able to chase you anywhere. I just wanted you to know that."

She tilted her head to one side. "Cavanaugh, you really provoke me. Don't you know by now that I'd love you if all you could do for the rest of your life is crawl around on your belly? If you can put up with my fresh mouth, the least I can do is overlook a cane or a limp."

He drove his fingers into her hair and held her head still while he kissed her ardently. "God, I love you."

"Well, hallelujah. I thought you'd never get around to saying it. And just for the record, I didn't pick up anybody in the Sugar Shack that night I went to Lahaina."

He had kissed his way down her chest. His lips were lightly plucking at her nipple. "I know."

"You know?"

"Hmm. We were well on our way to this by then. The only man you wanted that night was me." His nimble tongue traced damp patterns across her breasts.

Moaning and arching her back reflexively, she sighed. "Fairly confident of yourself, weren't you?"

"Not at all." It was a sacrifice, but he ceased what he was doing and looked up at her. "Falling off that mountain was nothing like falling for you, Lilah Mason. You know how Elizabeth is always saying I stay on the move, how I leave everybody breathless in my dust?" Lilah, mesmerized by the sincerity in his eyes, nodded dumbly. "Well, you not only slowed me down, you brought me to a skidding halt. And I'm not talking about when I was flat on my back unable to move. You toppled the mighty Adam Cavanaugh the first time he saw you in those irreverent black leather pants. From that moment on I didn't stand a chance, and I knew it. That's why I fought it so hard."

Lilah found it difficult to swallow and impossible to speak. He laughed softly. "Don't tell me I've rendered you speechless."

That prompted a smile and a wisecrack. "Hardly, Cavanaugh, but I'm tired of talking. You've got till the count of three to get this show underway."

"Or else what?"

She winked up at him. "Or else you've got till the count of four."

If you loved

ADAM'S FALL

don't miss this upcoming Bantam publication
of another heart-gripping romance by
New York Times *bestseller*
Sandra Brown

LONG TIME
COMING

a Bantam paperback on sale in December 1993.

*T*HE PORSCHE CREPT ALONG THE STREET LIKE A
sleek black panther. Hugging the curb, its engine purred so
deep and low it sounded like a predator's growl.

Marnie Hibbs was kneeling in the fertile soil of her flower
bed, digging among the impatiens under the ligustrum bushes
and cursing the little bugs that made three meals a day of them,
when the sound of the car's motor attracted her attention. She
glanced at it over her shoulder, then panicked as it came to a
stop in front of her house.

"Lord, is it that late?" she muttered. Dropping her trowel, she
stood up and brushed the clinging damp earth off her bare knees.

She reached up to push her dark bangs off her forehead before
she realized that she still had on her heavy gardening gloves.
Quickly she peeled them off and dropped them beside the
trowel, all the while watching the driver get out of the sports car
and start up her front walk.

Glancing at her wristwatch, she saw that she hadn't lost track
of time. He was just very early for their appointment, and as a
result, she wasn't going to make a very good first impression.
Being hot, sweaty, and dirty was no way to meet a client. And
she needed this commission badly.

Forcing a smile, she moved down the sidewalk to greet him,

nervously trying to remember if she had left the house and studio reasonably neat when she decided to do an hour's worth of yard work. She had planned to tidy up before he arrived.

She might look like the devil, but she didn't want to appear intimidated. Self-confident friendliness was the only way to combat the disadvantage of having been caught looking her worst.

He was still several yards away from her when she greeted him. "Hello," she said with a bright smile. "Obviously we got our signals switched. I thought you weren't coming until later."

"I decided this diabolical game of yours had gone on long enough."

Marnie's sneakers skidded on the old concrete walk as she came to an abrupt halt. She tilted her head in stunned surprise. "I'm sorry, I—"

"Who the hell are you, lady?"

"Miss Hibbs. Who do you think?"

"Never heard of you. Just what the devil are you up to?"

"Up to?" She glanced around helplessly, as though the giant sycamores in her front yard might provide an answer to this bizarre interrogation.

"Why've you been sending me those letters?"

"Letters?"

He was clearly furious, and her lack of comprehension only seemed to make him angrier. He bore down on her like a hawk on a field mouse, until she had to bow her back to look up at him. The summer sun was behind him, casting him in silhouette.

He was blond, tall, trim, and dressed in casual slacks and a sport shirt—all stylish, impeccably so. He was wearing opaque aviator glasses, so she couldn't see his eyes, but if they were as belligerent as his expression and stance, she was better off not seeing them.

"I don't know what you're talking about."

"The letters, lady, the letters." He strained the words through a set of strong white teeth.

"*What* letters?"

"Don't play dumb."

"Are you sure you've got the right house?"

He took another step forward. "I've got the right house," he said in a voice that was little more than a snarl.

"Obviously you don't." She didn't like being put on the defensive, especially by someone she'd never met over something of which she was totally ignorant. "You're either crazy or drunk, but in any case, you're *wrong*. I'm not the person you're looking for and I demand that you leave my property. Now."

"You were expecting me. I could tell by the way you spoke to me."

"I thought you were the man from the advertising agency."

"Well, I'm not."

"Thank God." She would hate having to do business with someone this irrational and ill-tempered.

"You know damn well who I am," he said, peeling off the sunglasses.

Marnie sucked in a quick, sharp breath and fell back a step because she did indeed know who he was. She raised a hand to her chest in an attempt at keeping her jumping heart in place. "Law," she gasped.

"That's right. Law Kincaid. Just like you wrote it on the envelopes."

She was shocked to see him after all these years, standing only inches in front of her. This time he wasn't merely a familiar image in the newspaper or on her television screen. He was flesh and blood. The years had been kind to that flesh, improving his looks, not eroding them.

She wanted to stand and stare, but he was staring at her with unmitigated contempt and no recognition at all. "Let's go inside, Mr. Kincaid," she suggested softly.

Several of her neighbors, who had been taking advantage of the sunny weekend weather to do yard chores, had stopped mowing, edging, and watering to gawk at the car and Miss Hibbs's visitor.

It wasn't out of the ordinary for a man to come to her house. Many of her clients were men and most of them consulted with her there. Generally they were stodgy executives in dark business suits. Few had deep tans, looked like movie stars, and drove such ostentatious cars.

This area of Houston wasn't glitzy like some of the newer neighborhoods. Most of the residents were middle-aged and drove sensible sedans. A Porsche on the block was a curious thing indeed. And to her neighbors' recollections, Marnie Hibbs had never engaged in a shouting match with anyone.

She turned on the squeaky rubber soles of her sneakers and led Law Kincaid up the sidewalk and through the front door of her house. Air-conditioning was a welcome respite from the humidity outside, but since she was damp with perspiration, the colder air chilled her. Or maybe it was her distinct awareness of the man behind her that was giving her goose bumps.

"This way."

She led him down a spacious hallway, the kind that could be found only in houses built before World War II, and toward the glassed-in back porch, which served as her studio. There she felt more at home, more at ease, and better able to deal with the astonishing reality that Law Kincaid had unexpectedly walked into her life again.

When she turned to face him, his arctic-blue eyes were darting around the studio. They connected with hers like magnets.

"Well?" he said tersely, placing his hands on his hips. He was obviously awaiting a full explanation for something Marnie was in the dark about herself.

"I don't know anything about any letters, Mr. Kincaid."

"They were mailed from this address."

"Then there's been a mistake at the post office."

"Unlikely. Not five times over the course of several weeks. Look, Mrs. uh . . . what was it again?"

"Hibbs. Miss Hibbs."

He gave her a swift, inquisitive once-over. "*Miss* Hibbs, I've been a bachelor for thirty-nine years. It's been a while since puberty. I don't remember every woman I've gone to bed with."

Her heart did another little dance number, and she took a quick, insufficient breath. "I've never been to bed with you."

He threw one hip slightly off-center and cocked his head arrogantly. "Then how is it that you claim to have mothered a son by me? A son I'd never even heard of until I got your first letter several weeks ago."

Marnie stared at him with speechless dismay. She could feel the color draining from her face. It felt like the world had been yanked from beneath her feet.

"I've never had a child. And I repeat, I never sent you a letter." She gestured at a chair. "Why don't you sit down?" She didn't offer him a seat out of courtesy or any concern for his comfort. She was afraid that if she didn't sit, and soon, her knees would buckle beneath her.

He thought about it for a moment, gnawing irritably on the corner of his lower lip before he moved to a rattan chair. He sat down on the very edge of the cushion, as though wanting to be ready to spring off it if the need arose.

Self-conscious of her muddy sneakers, ragged cut-offs, and

ancient T-shirt, Marnie sat in the matching chair facing his. She sat straight, keeping her dirty knees together and clasping her hands nervously on the tops of her thighs.

She felt unclothed and vulnerable as his incisive eyes moved over her, taking in her face, her uncombed hair, her yard work attire, and her grubby knees.

"You recognized me." He shot the sentence at her like a missile.

"Anybody who watches TV or reads a newspaper would recognize you. You're the most popular astronaut since John Glenn."

"And therefore I'm a visible target for every nut case who comes down the pike."

"I am not a nut case!"

"Then why the hell have you been sending me those letters? That's not even an original idea, you know. I get several dozen a day."

"Congratulations."

"They're not all fan letters. Some are hate mail from the religious crazies who believe we're going where God never intended man to go. Some credit God with the *Challenger* accident—His punishment for our tampering with heaven or nonsense to that effect. I've had proposals of marriage and of other assorted liaisons of a prurient and/or perverted nature," he said dryly.

"How nice for you."

Ignoring her snide remark, he continued. "But your letters had a stroke of originality. You were the first one to claim that I was the father of your child."

"Don't you listen? I told you I've never had a child. How could you possibly be the father?"

"My point exactly, Miss Hibbs!" he shouted.

Marnie stood. So did he. He tracked her when she moved to her drafting table and needlessly began rearranging sketch pencils and paintbrushes in their various canisters.

"You were also the first one to threaten me with public exposure if I didn't do what you wanted me to."

She turned to find him very close. She could even feel the fabric of his trousers against her bare legs. "What possible threat could *I* pose to you? You're the fair-haired child of the space program, hailed as a hero. You held every American spellbound in front of his television set while you and a Russian cosmonaut shook hands over a peace treaty in space.

"There was a ticker-tape parade in honor of you and your crew in New York. You had dinner at the White House with the President and First Lady. Almost singlehandedly you've turned around public opinion on NASA, which certainly wasn't favorable after *Challenger*. Critics of manned space flight are being ridiculed after what you've done.

"To pit little ol' me against a celebrity giant like you, I would have to be crazy or stupid. I assure you that I'm neither."

"You called me Law."

After her lengthy speech, his four-word rebuttal came as an anticlimax that took her off guard. "What?"

"When you first recognized me, you called me Law."

"Which happens to be your name."

"But the average man on the street would address me as Colonel Kincaid, nothing as familiar as Law. Unless we'd known each other well before."

She sidestepped that. "What did these alleged letters demand from you?"

"Money first."

"Money?" she exclaimed. "How crass."

"Followed by public acknowledgment of my son."

Marnie eased herself from between him and the drafting table. His closeness was wreaking havoc on her ability to think clearly. She began shuffling through a stack of sketches left lying on one of her worktables. "I'm a very independent, self-reliant person. I would never ask you or anybody else for money."

"This is a nice neighborhood, a big house."

"My parents'."

"They live here with you?"

"No. My father is dead. My mother suffered a stroke several months ago and is in a rest home." She slapped down the stack of sketches and faced him. "I manage to support myself. What business of yours is any of this?"

"I think the victim ought to get to know his extortioner." Huskily he added, "In every way."

His eyes moved over her again. This time more slowly and analytically. She saw them pause in the vicinity of her breasts, which the damp T-shirt did little to conceal. She could feel her nipples projecting against the worn, soft cotton and tried unsuccessfully to convince herself that the response resulted from the air-conditioning, and not Law Kincaid's stare.

"I'm afraid you'll have to excuse me now," she said with

affected haughtiness. "I'm expecting someone soon and I've got to clean up."

"Who are you expecting? The agency man?" At her startled expression, he said, "You mentioned him when I first got here."

"He has an appointment to look at my proposed sketches for a commission."

"You're an artist?"

"An illustrator."

"For whom?"

"For myself. I freelance."

"What project are you working on?"

"The cover of the Houston telephone directory."

His tawny eyebrows rose a fraction, impressed. "That's quite a commission."

"I haven't gotten it yet." Marnie could have bitten her tongue the minute the words were out. He was shrewd enough to catch the slip.

"It would be an important commission to you?"

"Of course. Now, if you'll—"

He caught her arm as she tried to go around him, headed for the front door. "It must get tough, living from one commission to the next while you maintain this house and pay your sick mother's medical bills."

"I do fine."

"But you're not rich."

"Not by a long shot."

"That's why you've been writing me these threatening letters, isn't it? To get money from me?"

"No. For the umpteenth time, I haven't ever written you a letter."

"Blackmail's a serious crime, Miss Hibbs."

"And a charge too ridiculous even to discuss. Now, please let go of my arm."

He wasn't hurting her. But his encircling fingers held her much too close to him. She was close enough to smell his sexy cologne and the minty freshness of his breath, close enough to see the dark centers of eyes that had sold more copies of *Time* than any other issue in history when they'd graced the front cover.

"You seem reasonably intelligent," he said.

"Should I take that as a compliment?"

"So why did you send anonymous letters to me, then put your return address on the envelope?"

She gave a soft, disbelieving laugh and shook her head. "I didn't. Or was that a trick question designed to trap me? Where are these letters? May I see them? Perhaps after I saw them I could offer an explanation."

"Do I look stupid? I wouldn't hand them over to you so you could destroy the evidence."

"Oh, for heaven's sake," she cried. Then, staring up into his stern face, she said, "You're really taking this seriously, aren't you?"

"At first I didn't. You were just one crank in hundreds. But after the fifth letter, when you got really nasty about pinning a paternity rap on me, I thought it was time to confront you."

"I'm not the kind of woman who would pin a paternity rap on any man."

"Even one with as high a public profile as me?"

"No."

"One who stood to lose a lot if there was a scandal?"

"That's right! Besides, I've told you that I've never had a child."

They heard the front door open, then bang shut. There were running steps in the hall. Then a tall, lanky teenage boy rushed through the door.

"Mom, you gotta come see the car parked in front of our house. It's totally *bad*!"

During the ponderous silence, Marnie listened to the knocking of her own heart. She tried to keep her face composed for the boy's sake, but it was difficult. After several seconds she hazarded a glance at Law Kincaid. He was staring at David. Disbelief was starkly evident on his handsome features.

It was David who finally spoke. "Jeez, you're Law Kincaid. Jeez!"

"David, I've asked you not to use that word."

"Sorry, Mom, but it's *Law Kincaid*. Law Kincaid in *my* house."

The astronaut replaced the incredulous expression on his face with his famous smile, his equanimity apparently regained. "David? Pleased to meet you." He stepped forward and shook the teenager's hand.

Across the room, Marnie gripped the edge of her drafting table for support. David was almost as tall as Law. His hair was the identical shade of blond, his eyes just as blue. He hadn't grown into his bones yet. They poked out like arrow tips at the shoulders, elbows, and ankles. Eventually, however, he would. The genetic blueprint had been drawn at conception. To know how he would look in twenty-two years, all David had to do was examine the man shaking hands with him.

Fortunately David was so starstruck to find the astronaut under his roof that he didn't notice the resemblance. Exuberantly he pumped Law's hand.

"I've got posters of the *Victory* in my room. Burger King was giving them away if you bought six Whoppers. I bought seven just in case. Would you autograph it for me? I can't believe this. What are you doing here? My birthday's still weeks away."

He looked at Marnie and laughed. "Is this the special present you've been hinting at? Oh, wait, I know. Did you talk him into posing? That's it, right?"

Law turned his back to the boy and faced her. His stare was as hot and blue as a flame. She quailed beneath it but kept her expression defiant. Law's expression was a mix of suspicion and puzzlement. "Posing?"

"I . . . I . . ."

"Uh-oh, did I let the cat out of the bag before she had a chance to ask you? Sorry, Mom." To Law, David said, "She's making a pitch to do the cover of the phone book. The other night she said she ought to get you to pose for the astronaut representing NASA."

"Hmm. Did she say why?"

"She thinks you're the best-looking, I guess," David said, grinning. "She knows you're the most famous."

"I see," Law said quietly. "I'm flattered."

"Will you do it?"

Law mercifully released Marnie from his stare and turned back to David. "Sure I'll pose. Why not?"

"Gee, that's terrific."

"It really isn't necessary," Marnie interjected. "I've already done a preliminary sketch." She gestured noncommittally toward the stack of sketches behind her.

"Let's see them."

"They're not ready for anybody to see."

"Don't you plan to show them to the adman?"

"Yes, but he's in the business. He knows the difference between a rough sketch and the finished product."

"So do I. And I'd like to see them." Law was issuing her a

challenge. Aware of David's curious eyes and knowing how perceptive he was, Marnie had no choice but to go along.

"Okay, sure." In contrast to her congenial voice, her smile felt brittle and breakable as she passed some of the sketches to Law.

"See, there you are!" David exclaimed, pointing down at the man's face in the montage of scenes depicting Houston. "Looks just like you, doesn't it?"

"It certainly does," Law said, giving Marnie another of those penetrating, inquiring stares. "Almost as though she knew my face intimately."

"She's good. The best," David boasted. "She even got the space suit right."

Marnie snatched the drawings back. "Since my drawings meet with your approval, there's really no reason for me to detain you, Colonel Kincaid. Thank you so much for stopping—"

The doorbell cut her off.

"I'll get it," David shouted, tearing off in that direction. Before he'd taken two steps, however, he braked and spun around. "You won't leave before I get back, will you?"

"No," Law told him. "I'll be here for a while."

"Great!"

The boy bounded down the hallway toward the front of the house, where the doorbell was being rung a second time.

Law closed in on Marnie and took her by both arms. In hushed but angry tones he hissed, "I thought you said you'd never had a son."

"I haven't."

"What do you call that?"

"I'm not his mother."

"He calls you mom."

"Yes, but—"

"And he resembles me."

"He—"

"But, dammit, I don't remember sleeping with you."

"You didn't! You didn't remember me on sight, did you?"

"Not on sight. But some things I never forget."

He yanked her hard against him. Before she could react, his lips were working hers open. His tongue breached them and dipped into her mouth. Opening his hand wide across her bottom, he tilted her hips forward and up against his.

A geyser of desire shot through Marnie.

Apparently Law was likewise struck.

His head snapped up and he looked at her with frank astonishment before pushing her away.

It all transpired within a matter of seconds, which was good since David was leading her most potentially important client to date down the hallway toward the studio.

By the time they reached it, Law was lounging against the edge of her desk, looking as innocent as a choirboy. She was standing in the middle of the room, feeling as adrift as if she were in the middle of the Pacific without a life raft.

"Mr. Howard," she said breathlessly, her fingertips on her throbbing lips, "please forgive my appearance. I was working in the yard when . . ." She gestured toward Law. "When Colonel Kincaid surprised us by stopping by."

She needn't have worried about him being put off by her disheveled appearance. He didn't even notice her. "Well, this is certainly an unexpected pleasure," he said expansively. The advertising agency executive stepped forward to shake the astronaut's hand. "It's an honor, sir."

"Thank you."

Only then did he acknowledge Marnie. "Ms. Hibbs, you didn't tell me you knew our latest national hero." Law's brows drew together into a frown. Clearing his throat uncomfortably, the man added, "No reason you should, of course."

"Colonel Kincaid's the model for her sketch for the phone book."

"*If* I get the job, David," she said, self-consciously wetting her lips. She tasted Law's kiss on them and experienced the outlandish but not unfounded fear that it might be visible. "Would you like to see the drawings I've made so far, Mr. Howard?"

"While you're doing that," Law said, "I'm going to take David for a drive."

"You mean in the Porsche?" the boy asked ecstatically. He let out an Indian war cry, leapt in the air, slapped the ceiling, and then raced from the room. "I've got my learner's permit, you know," he called back. "I'll get my license in just a few more weeks."

"David, don't you dare touch Colonel Kincaid's car," Marnie cried in alarm.

"He'll be all right."

"But where are you going?"

"Around the block," he said, giving a casual shrug with one shoulder. "No place special."

"How long will you be gone?"

"Awhile."

She wanted to scream at him for giving her vague answers. She wanted to put her foot down and say no, definitely not, David wasn't going anywhere with him. She wanted to run after David and grab hold tightly.

But with Mr. Howard standing there, she had no alternative but to be gracious. Knowing that, Law took full advantage of the situation. She watched him swagger down the hallway and out the front door to meet David, who was already sitting in the passenger seat of the car.

"Have you, uh, known Colonel Kincaid long?" Mr. Howard asked tentatively.

Marnie turned and saw that the man was dying of curiosity. He didn't have the nerve to come right out and ask about the relationship between the astronaut and the teenager who called her mom. Coolly she replied, "I've known him awhile."

Mr. Howard left twenty minutes later. She felt confident that he liked her preliminary sketches. He warned her, however, as he was zipping them into a large portfolio, that there were two other artists being considered and that the final decision would be left up to a committee of agency and telephone company executives.

"Your work is more avant garde than the other two."

"Is that bad?"

"No," he replied with a smile. "Maybe it's time we broke with the traditional." Beyond that all he would say was "You'll be hearing from us one way or the other in a week or so."

She walked him to the front door. Through the screen she watched him leave, at the same time scanning the street for a sign of the Porsche. It was nowhere in sight. Worriedly she wrung her hands. Where had they gone? What were they talking about? Was Law barraging David with questions he wouldn't know the answers to?

Before she worked herself into a tizzy, she decided to take a long overdue shower. Shortly she emerged from her second story bedroom dressed, wearing makeup, and feeling more self-assured than she had in cutoffs and T-shirt.

She was relieved to hear voices coming from David's bedroom. Stepping through the open doorway, she saw him listening, enthralled, to Law's description of the walk he'd taken in space.

"Weren't you scared?" David asked.

"No. By the time we got up there, we'd rehearsed everything so many times, I knew exactly what to expect."

"But something could have gone wrong."

"It could have. But I knew that I had a crew in the ship and another on the ground making sure that nothing did."

"What's it like when you blast off?"

Law squeezed his eyes shut. "Thrilling. Like nothing else. It's the culmination of tedious hard work, study, practice, delays, decision-making. But it's worth every second of the anticipation and frustration. More."

David inched closer. "What were you thinking?"

"Honestly?"

"Honestly."

"I was praying I wouldn't overflow my tee-tee bag."

David laughed. "No. Really?"

"Well, besides that, I was thinking, 'This is it. This is what I've always wanted to do. This is what I was born for. It's here. I'm living it.'"

"Gee."

The worshipful look on his face alarmed Marnie. "I hate to break this up," she said from the doorway, "but I've got to go to the rest home now. And, David, if you don't leave soon, you'll be late for soccer practice."

David rolled off his bed and landed on his feet. "Mom, you'll never believe this! He let me drive! That car is something else, almost like being in a cockpit, isn't it, Colonel Kincaid?"

"Almost. That's why I bought it. If I can't be flying, I want to pretend I am."

"It was terrific, Mom. You should've been with us." Then, looking guilty for being so caught up in his own excitement, he asked, "How'd your meeting with Mr. Howard go?"

"He liked my rough sketches but made no promises." Needlessly she consulted her wristwatch. "You'd better go, David."

"You play soccer?" Law had been sitting on the edge of David's bed. He came to his feet.

"I'm a halfback for the Tornadoes, my school team. We're going to be city champs."

"I like that tone of confidence," Law said with a broad smile.

"To make sure we win, the coach is working us double time."

"Then you'd better not be late for practice." They moved toward the door where Marnie was waiting.

"Will you be here when I get back?"

"No, he won't." When Marnie curtly answered the question that had been intended for Law, four identical eyes were turned on her. She gave a weak smile. "I'm sure Colonel Kincaid has other things to do, David. Run along now. But be careful on your bike. Got your house key?"

"Yes, Mom. Well, 'bye, Colonel Kincaid. I can't believe I got to meet you. Thanks for autographing my poster."

"It was my pleasure, David." They shook hands. For the first time that Marnie could ever remember, David seemed reluctant to go to soccer practice.

He trudged down the stairs, frequently turning his head to gaze back at Law. As soon as he was out the front door, Marnie looked up at her visitor.

"I really do need to leave for the rest home now. My mother's not doing well, and if I'm not there when she expects me, she—"

He blocked her path and checked the flow of superfluous words. The charm he had turned on for David had disappeared with the boy. "I want the truth from you. I want it now." He took a quick breath. "Is he my son?"

Her gray eyes filled with tears. Her tongue made a swipe at the lips now shiny with peach-colored gloss. She bowed her dark head so that the crown of soft curls almost touched the center of his chest.

"He's *my* son," she whispered. *"Mine."*

"Somebody fathered him." Crooking a finger beneath her chin, he tilted her head up. "Is he my son?"

Marnie looked directly into his eyes and answered, "Yes."

ABOUT THE AUTHOR

SANDRA BROWN is a former television personality and model who is married to her college sweetheart, Michael, a video producer. They have two children and live in Arlington, Texas.